Prisoners

Written By: Dawn Jaurequi

Chapter 1

The ugly girl

The ugly girl never gets the guy and when they manage to, they tend to lose them just as quickly. The ugly girl isn't respected, is invisible, will put up with far more than any other woman and all with a smile on her face, sure that this is the best that her life can offer. The ugly girl never hopes, never believes in fairy tales, never, absolutely never relies on anything pertaining to the manipulative powers of her femininity. She will work and work hard, will prove herself time and again, and will walk away if she feels threatened.

The ugly girl knows that she's ugly and never questions it, she just knows and deals with it, doing anything and everything she can do in order to keep the little attention that she manages to receive. Or, simply enough, learns to walk alone, trusting no one. The ugly girl sits in the back of the room, replaying in her mind every moment when someone has reminded her that she was ugly and unwanted, because, for some reason, ugly girls are reminded. Constantly.

That's where this story starts.

The ugly girl, that's me, sitting in the back of the room, of a local restaurant, waiting to hear, or rather hoping and praying that I get this job and am able to start tomorrow. Because, this ugly girl, upon hearing that her husband had cheated on her, yet again, decided to go out and get a job, a feat that it is nearly impossible after being a stay at home wife and mother for ten years. But, this ugly girl has been in the same town, as sinfully collapsing that it is, for all of forty years and after that time, there was bound to be someone that could give me an inside track on a job opportunity. And, sure enough there was: Mike and I went to High School together and, like the few of us that there are left, he just kind of stayed around in Elkton, watching it slowly fall apart.

Just one more person powerless to stopping the disaster that all of us knew was coming.

This would be a ghost town before long, or one of those tales of a good town turned prostitute drug crime area and looking more like an inner city than the small town we grew up in and loved. Most of us had managed to avoid the trappings of Elkton, most of us that is, Mike and I included in the few that managed to avoid the drugs and the prostitution, the crime and the lowering of our standards to fit into the atmosphere around us. While others we went to school with and grew up with took the road most traveled, throwing out the window all of the things each of us had been taught as children. Mike and I were from opposite sides of town, I was from the Manor, and still lived there, the seedy side of town with its own reputation, even twenty years ago, while Mike was from the rich side of town and both of us had managed to hold onto the principles our parents had instilled in us. Give to those that need it, feed those that are hungry, open your home and your heart to the many and the few will love and accept you, and always think of family first.

I hadn't seen Mike in years, he and his brother, John, were classmates of mine in High School. John was quiet and Mike was the jokester. Mike ran into me, a few days ago, when I had first found out about my husband's latest infidelity, as I was walking up the highway, just to be walking. I hadn't seen him in twenty plus years, and after crying on his shoulder, he told me he could get me a job.

That's what brings me here, sitting in the back of the room of his pizza place, situated on Route 40, just across the street from a cluster of fast food restaurants, apparently, this is his precious baby. He and his wife, Marie, never had children and this pizza place and all its employees are the closest thing they have to babies; hopefully, they adopt me as well so that I feel like I can finally leave that bastard I thought I could trust and thus married.

I am sitting here, in the best clothes I could find in my forgotten side of the walk in closet we have at home in the bedroom that was his and had never been mine. And, I'm praying that I get the job, despite the relationship that I have with God right now, since we're not really talking. When He's the One that told me to trust the one that I married and it turns out that I can't, it kind of disturbs any relationship that we had. The trust definitely weakens, if not wanes altogether. So, to be sitting here and praying is a long shot, but, it's all that I really have at the moment.

Anyway, people come in and people go, customers and friends, people that I know and some that I don't. Having been a stay at home mom for as many years that I have, I lose contact with the world and society and friends and the offspring of old classmates. As rewarding as it is, you tend to get older and life outside keeps going, and you wake up one day and realize that your life has been on pause all of this time. There's a little gray in your hair and you have the stretch marks from reproducing, proof that you just haven't been sitting around doing nothing, and you have weather and life worn wrinkles, and a heart full of regrets.

The heartbreak is just too much. And, that's when it starts.

The rapid heartbeat, the breath quick, the room spinning, and the surety that nothing will turn out the way it is supposed to. I can't see for a moment and I'm thinking about running away and not looking back, about abandoning the whole stupid idea in its inception. I look down at my hands and try to concentrate enough to count, keeping my eyes on my fingers and I suddenly realize my hands are shaking and my hands are old and wrinkled, looking much older than I am and I hide them under the table, unable to concentrate enough to bring myself down again.

Then, there's the next feeling, like a hand around my heart and my lungs and slowly squeezing. I can't breathe and I can't think and just then, Mike sits down at the table across from me and starts talking. It takes me a minute to realize that he's talking and I have to fight to snap myself out of it enough to hear and understand what he's saying. After several moments, I get it: I've gotten the job, dishwasher. I start tomorrow after the kids go to school. He's given me just enough time to walk up here from the Manor, after putting the kids on the bus and I'll get off about an hour before they get off of school. Part time, but, it's a job and I'm grateful for it, and I think I tell him that I am, but, I'm not sure.

I scribble my signature on several pieces of paper and stumble out of the restaurant, to a corner out front, up against the brick wall, out of the way and out of sight of anyone inside. There, I fumble through my backpack and find my cigarettes and light one with shaking hands. When I still can't come down, an anxiety attack feels like your grounded and suddenly snatched up to teetering on the side of skyscraper, sure that you're going to fall and having to be teetering, helplessly on the side, staring down at how far from the ground I really am, I, then, turn and face the brick wall. There, I stare and concentrate on the tiniest grains in the fake brick. I try talking to myself and nothing is working.

Then, someone speaks, a calming male voice out of nowhere:

"How long have you had them?" He asks.

"For a few years," I mumble.

That's when I feel something I hadn't felt in years. The sound of someone's voice was slowly inching me back down again from the ungodly heights in my emotions. I sigh heavily.

He asks, "Is there anything I can do?"

I smile, weakly, close my eyes, manage to take a drag off my cigarette and exhale before saying. "I know it sounds strange, but, keep talking."

"The sound of my voice is helping?" He asks, surprised.

"Yeah," I tell him, adding, "I've only known one other voice that can do that."

"And, who is that?" He asks.

"I married him," I say and laugh to myself, softly.

With the sound of his voice, I've inched my way down several stories and I'm nearly back on the ground, sure and stable again. But, I need him to keep talking. The shaking is slowly subsiding but the weariness is coming on quickly.

"Keep talking," I whisper.

"Right," he says, and then, "I've never met anyone like you before. You're quiet, willing to hide in the corner of the room and allow life to rush past you, giving everyone else a chance at the ride and applauding them for their success. When life is here for you, now, and you are cowering in the corner, hurt and unable to heal."

And, that's when I lost focus on the rest of what he was saying. You see, I had come down several stories and had this peaceful calm rush over me in an instant. He keeps talking and I am aware of people passing us and aware of the lines between the bricks, the feel of them beneath my fingers, the smell of pizza mixing with the all the other fast food restaurant smells around me, and the sound of the rush of cars going pass on the highway.

Soon, I am leaning against the brick, facing the parking lot and I'm smoking another cigarette, several butts at my feet, and I'm not sure o how long I've been there. But, I'm thinking straight again, realizing th need to get home soon and if I go there I'm sure Billy is with another woman or texting her, or something and suddenly there's a pain in my chest and the tears are threatening to come.

I turn to him, while he's still talking, and I say, in a quiet voice, "Thank you."

I walk away, head toward the highway, when I hear his voice behind me say, "I'll see you tomorrow."

I nod and think about all of the years that I've wasted on a man that could care less that I'm on the highway alone, fighting the urge to curl up in one of the tents I pass and cry and sleep this strange feeling off. For, the after effects of an anxiety attack is like being exposed and exhausted all at once and the need to sleep overwhelms you until you have to lay down and close your eyes. It's as though your mind has hit an override and you have to shut it down for a while. And, he doesn't care. Billy doesn't care. After all the years I've cared for him, gone door to door to beg for food and cigarettes, he's done this to me and he doesn't care of how much he's hurt me. He just tells me to get over it, like I can erase the pain and move on to the next pain that I know is coming, the next pain that he will inflict.

Yeah, the tents look comforting and inviting about now.

Then, there's the anxiety attack and the fact that another voice has managed to calm them the way only Billy ever has been able to. His voice stays with me and yet the details of his face allude me altogether. When you're having an anxiety attack, especially of how bad mine can be and have been as of late, there are details that completely slip past you unseen and unremembered. All I knew, after I was able to see and hear again, was that it felt as though there had been this intense conversation that I hadn't remembered. It's like I had had sex with him and hadn't even had the benefit of knowing the intense pleasure of why I was smoking.

What had been said?

All I remember is him saying that he had never known a woman like me before. I pass over the Route 40 Bridge, still envying the privacy of the tents off the side and hidden below, for just that one moment of being away from life as it is now, and I can't remember anything else that he said. I struggle to remember and end up allowing my mind to wander to my cheating husband and all that I am assuming that he is doing. With my head down and my thoughts drifting, I'm aware, only, of the rush of cars passed and the overwhelming feeling of being an exposed idiot out there for ridicule.

I cross over the bridge and take the next segment of walk, the long stretch by the shit plant, as though I can take it in leaps and bounds, even though my body is shaking and I have to clench my fists to ease their tremors. I hazard a look ahead and see our vehicle parked outside the liquor store and bar, just up ahead. Billy is behind the wheel and there's a woman leaning in the passenger window, shaking her ass and talking to him.

A pain hits me in the chest like I've been punched.

When you're the one that's been there and you've held all the promises and then suddenly you're not wanted anymore, the disrespect and the lies can be forgiven. But, the shit that's said in between the lies and the disrespect of the infidelity takes longer to heal. And, those voices of the one that can calm the anxiety attacks-*but now there is another voice*-becomes the haunting in your head and the reason why you can't stand life and people and walking and watching it continue. And, that's what's happening, it's continuing.

Despite the promises, despite the swearing, the haunting things said in between, and the declaration that everything is okay between us, it's continuing. She's nineteen and full of herself, blonde and thin and tiny, like she's miniature sized and he's telling me that he's staying away from her like she's this drug and he's the addict. And, sure enough, he's there buying and preparing to shoot up when it's convenient for him.

If only I could have his voice to replay when I need it, the mysterious voice that helped me outside of Mike's pizza place. If I could bottle it and carry it around, I could replay it when the next thunderous anxiety attack was to come, of which I can feel it coming now. My mental feet are no longer grounded and the feel of teetering on the side of another skyscraper is becoming apparent and real and uncontrollable. I can feel it coming and I'm walking right into the middle of the reason. I stop and look around, looking for a way out, someplace else to walk. But, since they've put the barriers up between the lanes of traffic on 40, you can't cross and escape such a scene like this one. I'm stuck.

"What do I do? What do I do?" I ask myself.

I stand for a moment, facing the traffic, the teasing voices in my head wanting me to take a haphazard step out into the lanes while the cars are accelerating from the light. And, I can't think of what to do. I try rummaging through my backpack and can't find my headphones. I can't even find my phone to plead with him to just take her off and out of my sight so that I can go home. So, yeah, I'm stuck, nowhere to go, and no way of stopping the inevitable from happening.

That's when a car pulls up, small, not overly expensive, classic in design, and fast. It stops right in front of me, pulling off the side of the road, the passenger side window slowly rolling down.

"Get in," the familiar voice says from the driver's side. "You didn't think I'd let you walk home alone, did you?"

"I," I stammer and can't think of anything witty to say or even an excuse to wave the car away. Honestly, I can't even think just then, so, I look around, taking one last look at Billy and his whore discussing details of their next rendezvous, if they hadn't already had it, and get in blindly and numbly. In the passenger seat, I close the door and buckle up. As he drives away, I watch Billy and our vehicle and the whore in the side rear view mirror become smaller and smaller until they're completely gone out of my sight.

"Where do you live?" He asks.

I sigh and can't stand the thought of having to pass Billy and her and I know that they'll be sitting there talking for some time. So, knowing that the kids won't be home for a few hours from school, I risk the unthinkable for a breathable moment.

"If you can, can you just drive?" I ask.

"Absolutely," he says, adding, "And, I know just where to go, someplace I haven't been in years, and someplace where you can relax for a little bit in the quiet."

At the light by Burger King, he turns right, and heads toward Chesapeake City on 213. I, honestly, don't care where we go, as long as I don't have to watch Billy and her and have to be reminded that I'm now the rejected one having to fake it all with a lovely little smile. I lean back into the seat and as he begins to ask how I'm feeling, my eyes, focusing on the road, and the exhaustion from walking after the anxiety attack all hit me at once and I doze off into a peaceful short sleep.

I wake, with a start, when the engine shuts off, and for a moment, I don't know where I am. Looking around, I smile to myself when I realize where we are. The sound of the water and the peacefulness of the quiet, no cars, no drug addicts, no hookers, no fighting, and no Billy and his whore around. And, suddenly, instead of being yanked to unbearable heights above, I'm yanked into the past.

"We're at the levies?" I ask, groggily.

"Yeah," he laughs, leaning the seat back and unbuckling his seat belt. "I haven't been here in years. The last time I was here, I was actually with you, if you remember. High school is a long time ago."

I try to think and the need for a cigarette to clear the fog outweighs the statement.

"Can I smoke in here?" I ask, digging out my cigarettes.

"Yeah," he answers and turns the key enough to put the windows down and turns it back again. In a moment, as I light up, he follows suit, complaining that it's a bad habit he wants to stop. While, in my head, I'm telling myself that smoking has kept me grounded, for the most part. I'm not a medication person and I need medication, I do. But, as far as I'm concerned, smoking is my medication.

"So, like I was saying," he repeats, "I haven't been here since I was here with you."

A few drags and the realization that I'm free from watching yet something else I can't bear to watch and I'm able to remember hit me and I am able to relax a little. And, then, I remember, able to focus on his words and relish the past that I've been yanked into.

It was my Junior Year, Mike had been giving me a hard time that day at school because my only real boyfriend had cheated on me with this whore that everyone had had in our high school. And, he told me to take a ride with someone that he knew, just to get away and think. He said to take the ride as a favor to him, because the driver was shy and awkward and had always wanted to talk to me but never could and the person would be going away the next day, to some music school or something. So, I had agreed, as a favor to Mike and ended up here, in this spot, crying on his shoulder and the shy girl that guarded her every ounce physically unfolded and relished the touches that followed.

But, I didn't unfold enough to get the first time I should have had. Just six months later came the rape that took my virginity and is at the heart of the anxiety attacks, like I went through a war zone and came out barely alive.

I sit back into the seat, sigh heavily and take another drag off my cigarette.

"Do you remember now?" He asks, teasingly.

"My God, John, how are you?" I ask and look over at him. The same blue eyes twinkle with his smile and the age of years survived unspoken pain shows in the wrinkles. But, beneath it all, he's still the sixteen year old that was too shy to talk to me, of all people, the ugly girl in the back of the room.

"Two divorces, a few kids, and I've missed you," he says, with a tiny smile.

"I've missed you," I tell him, not realizing that I'm smiling.

"So, how about you? What's happened since we were here last?" He asks.

"Well," I say, wanting to blurt out that six months after he left, I got a job, went to work and became the victim of the Store Manager, saying yes to sex, only to be slammed against the floor and forced anyway. I want to blurt out that I hid in the anxiety attacks for years, crying over the innocent boy that had held me and was gone, that I now felt too dirty to be near. I want to blurt out that by the time I emerged from the anxiety attacks, Billy was standing there, not really wanting me and forcing me to watch each and every one of his stops along the infidelity trail, emotional and physical both.

Instead, I tell him, "Bad stuff and then I had kids, and then more bad stuff." I couldn't tell him anything else. I had always been able to lie to everyone, until that day in his car. I just couldn't lie or hide anything from him, not even now, after all of these years gone.

"Does the bad stuff have anything to do with the anxiety attacks?" He asks.

"It does," I say.

He nods and asks, "Do you want to talk about it?"

"No," I say quietly.

"Right," he says, adding, "Then, we won't talk about it."

"Thank you," I whisper and that's when the sadness of all that never was hits me and the tears come. I cry, trying to fight the tears away behind my cigarette. But, the cigarette is gone and fight as I might, I can't light another one. Instead, I toss into the floor board, dejected.

"You know," he says, quietly, "I can't hold you when you're over there."

I laugh, through the tears, and tell him, "I'm too heavy to sit in your lap."

"I don't think you are," he says, winks at me and, reaching beneath the seat, pulls the lever that moves his seat all the way back from the steering wheel.

"I'm too big," I say, adding, "I don't want to hurt you, too."

He laughs, tells me, "You couldn't hurt me. I don't think you see yourself the way that you really are. My God, what is he doing to you?"

I look over at him, surprised, just as more tears come.

"Come here," he tells me.

And, blindly, I obey, tiptoeing through the mind field of a car you don't want to destroy on your way from moving from the passenger seat to the driver's seat. There, I sit in his lap, one foot between the door and the seat and my other foot in the tiny space between the middle console and the seat. He smiles and leans back, relaxed.

He says, "See, you're not hurting me." He opens his arms as more tears come and, not wanting to, I wrap my arms around him and cry.

After several long moments in tears and his arms holding me, he teasingly says, "See, just like old times." I laugh. In the midst of a very painful explosive tearful episode, after having come down from the height of an anxiety attack, shaking and exhausted, he gets me to laugh.

I lean back, still laughing, wiping the tears away.

And, that's when he reaches up, places one hand behind my head and pulls me into him for a sweet, shaking kiss. He stops, as though he's afraid that he's crossed a line in the sand that I've drawn and looks at me for some cue of what to do now. And, I can't help myself. I can't. It's been so long since I've had any kind of contact, that I can't get enough. I grasp the seat behind him and dive in, devouring his lips like I've been starving, which I have been. When I realize that I've just crossed that same invisible line, I stop, lean back, out of breath. He watches me for a moment and nods.

John says, quietly, with anger in his voice, "I'm going to kill him."

Chapter 2

Haunting

I'll kill you and dispose of your body and no one will come looking for you.

-you have my innocence, what more do you want?

He doesn't want you, I don't even know why you thought anyone would ever want you.

He's fucking around on you and no wonder, it is you we're talking about.

I don't know why anyone would ever want to be with you?

-yes, mom, yes, I hear you, yes, you're right, mom, whatever.

You're just so fucking stupid, do what I tell you to do and nothing more, nothing less.

-why can't you just go away?

I can't have sex with you, I just can't. I'm not going to, so you can stay.

But, that's it between us. There will be no sex.

You can give me what I want, but, I will not give you what you want.

-so, I'm a prisoner now, is that what you're telling me?

She's just so tight, I can't stay away from her.

You're just going to have to understand, this isn't about love.

I don't love her, I love you.

But, I'm not stopping what I'm doing, I want to have sex with her.

-how can you love someone and not want them?

You've never been worth anything anyway.

You can't even take care of your responsibilities.

You are just like your father.

-yes, mom, yes, mom, I hear you.

I want to be with you, not be with her, but it's only sex, babe.

Don't you get that, just sex?

We just can't have sex anymore.

But, you, well, no one is going to want you with you loaded down with three kids.

So, you want to stay together, this is the way life now is.

-I sacrifice my sex life and you do not.

You were just so busy with the kids and all.

I wanted to make your life easier.

-by getting a girlfriend?

Not a girlfriend, not really, just sex, babe.

Nothing more than that.

What we have is so much more important than sex with her.

-than stop

But, I just need to do this.

Why can't you just be happy for me?

I mean, I've sacrificed so much.

-like what? Money in order to screw that whore?

You just don't get it.

You don't.

I thought you loved me, understood me, got that I have to do certain things.

-like lie and cheat

If you were just better.

I don't know, the kids have played havoc with you and I'm just not feeling it anymore.

-now it's the kids fault and mine

You know, she's just tiny and I need this.

-and not me

Be happy for me, why can't you be happy for me?

Just once a week, maybe twice.

Well, I have gone without painless sex for so long that maybe three times a week.

-why don't you just share her tent?

You're just heavy on my back.

-why didn't you tell me that?

You're just, I don't know, I don't feel anything with you in bed anymore.

-now, it's me again

It was about time.

I don't know, we just couldn't spend time together.

With your mom and the kids, you just weren't there.

I had to do this for me.

Just understand, this isn't about you.

This isn't about you.

-it is, though. . .can't you see, that it is. . .

Chapter 3

The starving girl

When you're hungry, it doesn't matter what you run across in the refrigerator or cabinet, you'll eat what you find and pay the consequences later. When you're hungry, and you just happen to run across that favorite snack that you've been hiding, well, then, that's a completely different story altogether. Even though you may be on a fast, or committed to a diet of some sort, the moment you find a cheeseburger, the diet can wait. You'll get back to the diet tomorrow, or the next day, depending on how scrumptious that fucking cheeseburger just happens to be.

But, wait, did I say hungry?

Try starving.

Now, that's another thing altogether.

I take agreements and commitments seriously. And, when I agreed that I was marrying Billy, ten years ago, I agreed that he was the only one that I would have sex with. And, if we weren't having sex, I wasn't having sex with anyone else. Little did I realize that he's interpretation of that agreement was that if I wasn't having sex with him, than, well, he would just find someone that would. Even if he had to pay her in order to perform the act, or rather have it performed on him.

And, still I remained faithful.

But, you place a starving girl in the arms of someone she has missed and she's allowed to cry on that trusted shoulder, when she has no one else in the world that she can trust, well, I guess she feeds and feeds and feeds. I'm not trying to excuse away all that happened. But, I'm just explaining that I am loyal, I am. I'm just so damn lonely and sad and, what is it that I am?

Broken. Yeah, that's it, I'm broken.

I couldn't stop kissing John, I couldn't. I hold on to the seat behind him and lean into each and every kiss. Long before Billy's infidelity, he would reject me and I'd beg for his attention, only to have the rejection even louder. Until, I just slept on the couch without being looked for, without him coming to find me anywhere. It was like I was missing and he was going on with life as usual. Nothing different. Nothing else mattered but finding that attention online and playing his mental and emotional games elsewhere.

That's it, I'm broken.

I can't expect anyone to pick up the pieces when I'm not sure what's happened to them all. It's been so long since the shattering began that I'm not sure which room to even search first. I'm not even sure that there's any pieces that can be recovered now. I wonder if I'm just all dust now, no pieces to be salvaged, and the slightest wind can just blow it all away.

That's why I'm sitting in John's lap and pressing myself closer to him, relishing the way his hands are creeping under the back of my shirt and teasing my spine. That's why I'm sitting here, listening to the delightful sounds of heavy breath and the water and the sounds of bugs playing in their safe places. Unseen and unhindered.

The couch is a memory, at this moment. And, the pain in my chest, that pounding that finds its way to my ears, is suddenly silent and distant. If only he had attempted to find me, our home isn't that big to where you can't locate the couch in the living room. If only he had thought of me before acting, talked to me, made an effort to save what we have. If only and all of the possibilities fly around like annoying mosquitoes that don't stay, finding some other place to roam.

At this moment, I am broken but I am alive.

With every touch, I am reminded that I am human. I am not a servant, imprisoned in a house, caring for a man that doesn't care if I show up for work or not. Because, there's always someone else like me out there, somewhere, for the right price. The problem is, my price has always been far too low. One kind word every few years and I work, once again, until I prove that the next kind word isn't for naught.

With every touch I am female. I am a woman and attractive and wanted, even if only for the moment. And, all I need is this moment. Please, just allow me this moment. Because here, stuck in this moment, imprisoned here, I can face all the damage that is occurring and mentally be able to face it over and over and over again. Here, I am feminine. I am not a factory recall. There is nothing wrong with my sex. I am good enough. I am active and alive. I am protected and reminded that I am, too, a sexual creature.

Because I am. I am a sexual creature. Since finding out about her, I haven't even been able to be self-gratifying in any way. I've been so broken and disgusted that I am just nothing. That's it, I've felt like less than nothing, even alone. Even the fantasies wouldn't work. All I would see were every detail of moments Billy shared with her that I never saw with my eyes but could dictate to you verbatim. And, the images sent me time and again into a state of anxiety and panic, wanting to run and staying only for my boys.

But, here, now, I am alive and I don't want this moment to end.

And, my God, being near John again, reminded me of my youth. Of all that I had lost as a teenager. Most teenagers have the backseat fumbling and the first time moments, where you think you're in love just because it's the first moment that you have gotten close with anyone. I never had that, outside of being with John that day, much too long ago, and here he is when I need him and I don't want to let go.

But, I have to.

I am still married. Faithful to the unfaithful, imprisoned to the one that gives crumbs to me and full course meals to his whore. To the one that is youthful and knows the power of her youth from having used it against all the married women that have come before me, leaving me powerless to even fight her. But, I decided to stay. And, everything that happens after that decision is my responsibility because I agreed to stay. I agreed to put up with Billy and his nonsense, agreeing that this is the way I allow my life to continue.

Doing this, now, no matter how much I need it and want it and, my God, would trade nearly all of the world for it right now, would just make me just as guilty as Billy. And, I can't do that. Not to my boys. Not to myself.

I grip the back of the seat and yank myself out of the sweet fall that was that kiss. I break away and, out of breath, lean my forehead against his.

He says, "You can't do this, I know."

"I'm sorry," I plead.

"No," he says. "I'm sorry because I just want to fucking kill him right now."

I nod.

That's not the first time I've heard that in that past few months. And, apparently, it won't be the last time that I'll hear it. Nonetheless, I chose to stay. Why, I'm still not sure. And, how much longer I can endure, I don't know.

But, the morsel that is this moment, all I know, is that it isn't enough.

It has to be, but, it's not.

I can't move. And, I hold on, wanting to say something profound and something meaningful that will leave an impression or make the moment as much to him as it is to me, but, I can only think of:

"Thank you. I, I don't know how to explain, but, thank you."

Without saying anything, he grabs hold of me in a loving embrace and doesn't let go for long moments. His hand is on the back of my head and his face is buried in my hair and he doesn't want to let go. And, I don't want to be released. I've composed myself. The holding has allowed the excitement to relax and my heavy breath becomes peaceful. I can sleep here. I can live here, stay here forever.

Then, he says, "You are worth more than this."

And, manages, in that tiny heartfelt sentiment, to fuck up my composure.

I shake my head slightly. He holds onto me tighter.

He repeats, "You are worth more than this."

I shake my head again. The tears escape and I try to fight them away.

"You are worth more than this."

I hold on tighter as more tears come. I've only cried, as of late, to the point to where the outer layer just releases and the inner pain hasn't been touched. Much like releasing a pressure valve on the pain, just enough to be functioning and nothing more. In order to heal, I'd have to scream and cry and fight and the thought of the sobs that would escape frightens me, and now they slowly emerge.

"You are worth more than this, baby. Do you hear me? You are worth more than this."

I collapse, hold onto him for life in the drowning, and scream into his shoulder. He holds me tighter, running his fingers through my hair.

One more time, he says: "You are worth more than this. Listen to me, you are worth more than this, at least you are to me. Even if you don't believe it for yourself, that you are worth more. You are worth more to me. There hasn't been a moment when I haven't thought about you, wished I was with you, asked about you, and dreamed of seeing you again. You are worth more than this. You are worth more than this."

John holds me until the surge of pain subsides and I am so relaxed in his arms that my eyes close involuntarily. I dream, that's how peaceful and deep the sleep is, that I dream. I dream of laying on the beach and laughter in the background and I think the laughter is someone else's, but, every time I ask who is laughing the laughter stops. And, John's voice tells me that it's my laughter. It's been so long since I've heard the sound of my own laughter that it sounds foreign and strange to me.

I wake with a start.

"The boys," I say, startled.

He laughs, presses my head back against his chest and tells me, "I'm watching the time, you're alright. We still have time. Everything is okay. If you need to sleep, sleep. Because I don't think you've been sleeping, have you?"

"No," I tell him.

"Sleep, then," he says. "Even with you asleep, you're still here and safe and not being tortured by that asshole."

I drift off to the feel of his breathing and the smell of his cigarette smoke. His hands through my hair relaxes me further. I'm just tiptoeing in the water at the beach, happy and content, taking the walk, with the colors so brilliant and real that I can almost taste them.

Then, he says, "Do you know that you talk in your sleep?"

Groggily, I ask, "Do I?"

"Yeah," he laughs, "You do and it just makes me want to fucking kill him all the more. How can he expect you to believe that he loves you and make you watch him going out and fucking her? Is he really paying her?"

"Um hmm," I mumble.

I'm so peaceful, so relaxed that I don't notice that I've put my guard down in more ways than I ever intended. It just feels so good to be here now and I just need this: my oasis in the nothing.

"God, he's fucking stupid," he tells me.

"Mm," I manage to say, and nothing more.

He leans his head against mine, runs his fingers through my hair and says, "Sleep, we still have time."

Sometime later, I wake, after a short dreamless sleep and I rub my head against him, lovingly. I feel more than hear him laugh.

"I've missed you," he says.

I want to tell him that I've missed him. Instead, I lean back, cradle his face with my hands and press my lips against his. He smiles.

"Enough said," he laughs.

I press my forehead against his and proceed to have a laughing moment where I attempt to untangle myself and reach the passenger seat again. I am getting older and my legs and feet don't want to cooperate and the laughter that comes between the two of us, his hands roams a little in the helping teasingly, is like drinking. I am drunk on that laughter. And, I hold onto it for dear life, remembering what I would facing just moments from now.

"I don't want to go," I tell him.

"I know," he says, adding, "But, don't worry, I'm not going anywhere and there'll be more moments like this one. There will be. You have to get the kids and just concentrate on them, okay."

I nod.

"Listen," he says, "I know it isn't enough to help or anything, but, just listen to me, because I've been as stupid as he is now. He'll make you feel guilty like you've done something against him or something. Like what's happened here was something that you've done wrong."

And, that's when the guilt starts. He's right, he is, and yet, I still see it as doing something wrong. Billy will use it to turn the light off of him and unto me, like I'm the one that should be guilty and he would need something in exchange for what I've just done.

How the hell does he know this?

"And," he continues, concentrating on the steering wheel, "You may not be talking to God and I can understand why, but, God doesn't blame the hurting. God doesn't hate you and isn't punishing you for anything. What happens when you're abused is that the abuser will make you feel like everything has happened because of you and not them. They won't take responsibility for their own actions. They won't, they'll keep throwing it back onto you and expect you to just shake off the impossible, while they can't ignore the little things that you need."

I think for a moment and ask, "Why are you telling me this?"

"Because, right now," John tells me, "I want to save you. But, I'm pretty sure that you won't take it even if it were offered to you. Right now, you have something to prove to everyone else and to yourself and I'm just here, I'm not leaving. So, I'm not going to scoop you up and rescue you, but, I refuse to leave this time."

"Why?" I ask.

"You are my 'the one that got away,'" he tells me. "And, I don't want to lose you again."

"What is it with the one that got away?" I ask.

John laughs. "I don't know," he tells me, "but, just know that I don't want to go anywhere."

I take a breath and feel like the only thing that I've been waiting for is slipping through my fingers as quickly as I've managed to grasp hold of it. I can't do this and it's not really mine, I think all at once. I'm not diving in head long just to lose him again, just to lose something and someone else.

"Look," I tell him, "I may be hurting right now and be going through this unbearably strange thing, but, I'm not a teenager anymore. And, I feel old and tired and discouraged, I guess. And, I'm not holding onto something that only has its roots in the past. You don't know me anymore. And, from what I understand about the person that isn't sleeping with me, you wouldn't want to."

John takes a breath, a heavy thick one, head bent back to the roof of the car, and shakes his head. He closes his eyes. I watch him, unable to say or do anything, wondering what the hell he is doing, what the hell is happening.

He opens his eyes, looks back to the steering wheel, running his hands over it, thoughtfully. He shakes his head again and sits back in his seat, heavily.

"I have so much work to do," he says, to himself, lighting up another cigarette.

"What did you say?" I ask.

He exhales, says, glancing over at me, "I have so much work to do."

I shake my head. I feel myself getting angry. Embarrassed. That's how I feel, all at once, embarrassed, like I'm a mental case and he has to relegate me to the couch. Or, I'm working at his job now and need his training.

"What work do you have to do?" I ask, through clenched teeth, lighting a cigarette.

"I can hear the anger in your voice," John says. "Please, don't take it that way. I'm not here to train you, good God, what the fuck does he think he is to treat anyone like this? It's not that, honey, it's not. And, I'm not a teenager anymore, either. I just want to see where this path can go. Sometimes, people aren't ready to walk the path together. And, it takes time before they are. Maybe we just needed time and we've had it and now I like being with you."

He looks over at me, studies me for a minute, and says:

"I just want to spend time with you," he tells me.

I nod and say, "Why would you want to?"

"Because I do," he says, with a little smile.

"What about this work that you have to do?" I ask, sarcastically.

"Well," he says, starting the car and putting it into gear, "You don't see yourself the way that you are. You are beautiful, centered, a raging storm right now, but, you know who you are, at least for the most part. But, he's lied to you so much that you just don't see everything that you are."

"And, you do?" I ask.

He smiles, while we buckle up and he pulls out of the hole that we were parked in, and off down the dirt road, leading back to Chesapeake City and back towards Elkton.

John says, "I still see the shadow of the sixteen year old that I held in the beautiful woman that I held onto today. And, trust me, I held back. I did. If I didn't hold back, you'd be in a bed right now, still being touched and well."

That's where he stops.

I laugh and tell him, "Thank you, it's been a long time since" and my voice trails off and I can't finish my sentence.

"Since you've been wanted?" He asks.

"Yeah," I say, in a whisper.

He nods, tells me, "That would be part of the work that I have to do, wouldn't it?"

"I guess so," I tell him and reach over and touch his hand.

Before I am able to take my hand away, he grasps hold of it and holds it tight.

"I'm not going anywhere," he says, "I swear. I'll see you tomorrow. If you need me tonight, call the store. Mike and Marie are there constantly. And, they'll let me know. Okay?"

I nod.

He drops me off near where he picked me up. And, when I got out of the car, he winks at me and brushes his hand across his heart. He's angry, I can see it, angry, I think, that he has to drop me off to return to Billy and all that I'm now facing. Angry, even, a thought teases the corner of my mind, that he held back when he would have preferred to jump in right away, doing all that he thinks that I need.

And, I do need so much more than what happened.

I smile and wave as he speeds away.

Billy is nowhere to be seen and I'm able to walk home without the worry of another anxiety attack. The guilt, though, feels like carrying luggage and I wonder if Billy felt this way when he started fucking his latest whore. And, just as the wonder appears, I destroy it, that's the last thing I need to do right now: feel sorry for him. I've spent ten years feeling sorry for him and right now I need to heal and stand on my own two feet and be the person that even God would want me to be.

And, the person that I am right now isn't that person.

I walk home, into the neighborhood, and get to the bus stop in plenty of time to pick up the boys. They are smiling and happy and as I walk them back to the house, they give me a rundown of their day. What breaks my heart, though, is when they ask if I'm okay.

Apparently, try as I might, I haven't been able to hide from them my pain.

I reassure them and open the door. They go in ahead of me and I make their snack and pick up a few things around the house before starting dinner. When they've ventured off to play and play their video games, Billy comes into the dining room and tells me that he saw me get into a car.

Then he asks, "Where have you been all this time?"

I lie and he knows I'm lying and for the rest of the night, he's relentless. I'm guilty and because of my guilt and the punch on the brick wall that he did, I now owe him and he has to see her, despite the fact that he was setting up the meeting anyway. And, on and on and on. I try to stop him, reassuring the boys and at one point he gets the boys to make fun of me and the only reason I don't fall completely apart is because of the moment that I was able to have that day.

Because of John, I keep it together.

I manage to make dinner, get the boys ready for bed, and even have time to sit down and relax. And, in the midst of it, Billy continues, never giving me a moment of peace. That's when I see him, for the first time, of what he really is: a big, overgrown child, throwing a temper tantrum. I've suddenly have had enough. It's near midnight, with the boys asleep, that he punches the brick wall, when I refuse to give into his temper tantrum and allow him to go off with her. I didn't even deny him the right. I just simply ignored him, hiding in the moment earlier that day. It's amazing what you can do when you need to mentally distract yourself.

After he punches the brick wall and messes up his hand, I tell him, "Right, now what have we learned from this?"

It was a rhetorical question after all and the fact that he doesn't answer is beside the point. There was no real answer to the question. But, the question did need to be asked.

Chapter 4

Manipulation

You are the liar.

We had an agreement.

-did we now?

You got into the car with someone.

Where did you go?

-why would you care?

You owe me now.

I'd say no complaints and I do what I want.

-aren't you doing that anyway?

You don't fucking care.

Who the fuck would want you anyway?

-at least I'm not paying for anything

What the fuck were you doing?

About your job, right.

Who the fuck said that you could get a job anyway?

-I don't remember asking

So whoring yourself around again, are you?

Yeah, that's who I married, a fucking whore.

I knew I married a whore.

And, it's no wonder that I do what I've been doing.

    -right, I haven't had sex in over a year, but, I'm the whore

So, yeah, you're not giving me pussy.

I knew you had to be giving it to someone else.

    -right, I can't even take care of myself right now, sexually

So I'm not allowed to lie but you are?

That's nice, double standards we are playing, huh?

      -is that the name of the game you're playing?

I knew he didn't love you.

I mean, how could he love you?

No one else does.

      -right mom

So, what do I get for your lying episode?

Do you want me to call the store and get the truth of where you were?

     -sure, you'll have to figure out which store first

I can find out the truth.

You're not good at lying.

                              -unlike you?

I am the master and you cannot fool the master.

And, let me tell you I'll take the kids.

I will.

And, I'll put you on the mental ward of the hospital.

So, don't play this game with me.

I will win.

Chapter 5

The working girl

The working girl can be what is typically known in areas where there are hot and heavy as a hooker or streetwalker or prostitute. But, then again, a working girl is also those women that yank their asses out of bed, get ready for work, while cleaning the house and taking care of the kids, and then after putting the kids on the bus, turn around and walk up the highway to their job. That, in my opinion, should be considered a working girl. Those others are leeches. But, that's my opinion, coming from a wife and mother that has been good to her old man and fought to keep him alive, only to see the little money we have go flying out the window to one of these leeches to aid their heroin addiction.

Anyway, a working girl can juggle more balls than she has time to count. She drags her ass to work, even when the world is falling down around her ears. She takes no shit, unless it's at work, and there she reminds herself that she's got kids to take care of and bills to pay. She's not like the other workers, young and with no responsibilities, some of them only working to get their first paycheck so that they can buy their dope and get high. She will put up with shit that those other workers won't, putting her head down and just doing. She will work and work her ass off to prove herself, complaining only when the time comes for her to go home.

Because, of course, she has other responsibilities that need tending to.

That's me, the working girl now. And, for several weeks, that's what I did, got up every morning, dragging myself out of bed after a night of not sleeping, sometimes because of Billy and other times because of my illness. Yes, the road to recovery is admitting you are sick. I am sick and I don't see how you can recover from something like this. Nonetheless, I put my head down and worked. I carried dishes and operated the dishwasher, cleaned and organized, and never complained.

For several weeks, that's how life was.

John and I saw each other, but, we passed merely for those three weeks and nothing more. He'd give a supportive touch on the back, here and there, but, no words were passed between us. I guess it was enough, in his eyes to see me every day and know that I was alright. And, to know, too, that for three weeks, I didn't have a single anxiety attack.

Not one.

Life was good and looking up and several roads had opened for me and I really didn't care what Billy did or who he managed to pay to do it with. No, I honestly thought that above and beyond everything else that this is how my life could be and would be: anxiety free, no illness, and happiness, despite the misery at home. For several weeks, I was in denial and happy and sure that nothing could change that.

Billy never knew where I was working, but, after three weeks, he kind of figured it out on his own. The master, you know, likes to follow his faithful wife around once he thought that she was cheating and was so damn eager to take her boys from her and put her on the fourth floor of the hospital.

So, yeah, he follows me.

I walk up the highway to go to work and I know that he's following me. But, I'm so damned tired of his nonsense, knowing he's still fucking her and still wanting this perfect little life at home with me, his servant and the outward sign of all his fakeness. I shake my head and keep walking. Every time he passes, he doesn't even blow the horn, just drives passed and circles around, up one side of the highway and down the other and back again, over and over and over again until I reach the light at 40 and 213. There, he turns unto 213 and parks in the parking lot opposite the Burger King, to watch where I'm going.

That's the only thing he does that is intelligent. With all of the driving, all I keep thinking about is even more money just draining out the window in gas. All to see what I'm doing and where I'm going. Like I'm the one that needs to be watched and kept an eye on. Like I'm the one that needs to be followed, like I am the one that can't be trusted.

I walk pass him and don't even look at him. And, he has the nerve to throw up his arms like I was supposed to come running to the driver's side of our vehicle and talk to him. What else did he want me to do? Shake my ass and put a goofy smile on my face? Or, better yet, jump around, nod off, or complain about being sick?

Yeah, that job belongs to his whore. Not me.

I walk pass, cross one parking lot and then another and go inside Mike's pizza place. I head straight toward the back, passing John, and raising my eyebrows and shaking my head at him. John gets the hint and goes to the front door to look out. Over my shoulder, I see him shake his head and go outside to smoke.

I go in the back and start my shift early.

Mike comes into the tiny closet type room that is my work station.

"Everything okay?" He asks.

"Yeah," I lie to him.

"Look, Ronnie, my brother is worried about you," he says. "I know he's worried because he's outside pacing and taunting your old man."

"What?" I ask, dropping a plate on the floor.

I bend down to pick up the pieces and tell Mike, over my shoulder, "I'm sorry. Look, all I want to do is work and I'm here to do that. And, your brother means a lot to me, he does and I don't want to be the cause of anything happening, because I'm not worth it, I'm not and I know that I'm not and he should find someone better and I don't want anything happening to him."

When I stand and I run out of things to say in my ramble, Mike is laughing.

"It's cool," he says, adding, "I just want to know what to tell the cops if I have to call them."

I laugh a little and nod, saying, more to myself, "Let's hope it doesn't come down to that."

"Yeah," Mike tells me, "Because, my brother doesn't look like it, but, Billy wouldn't survive that."

I dump the pieces of the broken dish in the trash can and apologize yet again.

"Don't worry about the dish," he tells me, "My grandmother died a few months back, a bitter old woman that no one liked in the family. She liked me and left me with an entire store room of dishes. I don't know, don't ask. I can't figure it out either."

I laugh and before Mike walks away, I tell him, "I'll go out and drag John back in. He doesn't need to be getting into the middle of this."

And, I don't need to be on the fourth floor of the hospital tonight.

"Thank you, Ronnie," he tells me.

But, there's one more thing.

"Mike," I call him back, "Can you answer me a question?"

"Yeah," he says.

"Why is John," and I lose all train of thought.

"I'll answer the question you can't ask," he begins, "By saying that if I had been through all that John had been through and I found you again and I knew what you were going through, all I'm saying is that I would take my time and you would never have to live in the dark again."

And, with that, he's gone.

I take a minute, shake my head, and walk out front. I'll let what Mike has said sink in later, because at this moment, I just don't believe it, any of it to be true at all. So, rather than allowing it to eat away at my brain, I walk to the front and out into the restaurant. There, I survey the scene.

Billy is now sitting, still behind the wheel in Mike's parking lot and he and John are yelling at one another. I think and come up with something that may work if I do it right. Anything to remove John from the firing line. I'm not one of those women that get off on being in an abusive relationship and both teasing the abuser with the new man and thus asking to be beaten again. No, I'd rather deal with this bullshit alone.

Because, unlike them, I'm sure I don't deserve the attention.

So, having had written in my journal the night before, a simple poem, I think that if I write it and place the piece of paper against the window, in just the right angle to where Billy can't see, it will attract John's attention and get him back inside. I find one of the waitress' pads, take a page, and scribble a couple of lines on the back. I ease my way up to the brick that stands between the two sets of double doors, right next to where John is standing and yelling, cigarette burning in his hand and his face flaming red.

I knock on the glass. Nothing.

I knock again, this time slightly harder on the glass. Still nothing.

"Damn it, John, come on," I whisper, and knock again.

This time he turns around and steps close to the glass. I hold up the handwritten few poetic lines for him to read. He takes a minute, reads them, closes his eyes, and leans his head back. He turns back toward Billy, throws out his cigarette amid the taunting and walks back inside, stopping just in front of me.

John looks down at me, reaches over and takes the piece of paper, reads and rereads it again and folds it up neatly and places it in his back pocket. He looks at me for a moment longer, looks away, and leans in close to me.

That's when he says, "I swear to you I will fucking kill him."

And, he walks away.

I see him for a few hours that day and then, he's gone. Just gone.

I work my shift and keep an eye on the door and still there is no John. Billy stays outside for an hour or so after I had managed to get John inside and then he was gone and never returned. At the end of my shift, I clean up, hand the reigns over to my very young night shift worker and shake my head at how high he is coming into work, and leave.

With my backpack slung over my shoulder and a cigarette in hand, I walk home. I manage to get to the bridge on 40 and I see a tent and that's when the thing that had been missing for three weeks appears. And, it appears with vengeance. My knees buckle and I fall on the side of the highway, with images of desperation and pain so severe I can't find escape. A familiar car pulls up, just as I am forcing myself to stand and trying desperately to get my breath again. I have to walk home, there is no other way. But, the figure from the car that had disappeared that day half carries me and half drags me inside. There, he shuts my door and climbs into the driver's side before speeding away into traffic.

"You can't keep doing this, Ronnie," John tells me.

"I know, I'm sorry," I tell him.

"Do you understand them at all?" He asks.

"I think this one was the fact that you were just gone," I tell him, not wanting to sound weak and my knees throbbing from the impact on the asphalt.

"I'm sorry, Ronnie, fuck, I'm sorry," he tells me.

I nod and apologize again.

He veers into the turning lane, to take 40 back down in the direction I had been walking.

"I'm sorry I ran off today," he tells me, adding, "I just needed to walk away. I won't hurt you and I know that guys will say that when they want something. I know that because I've done it, but, it's not like that, I swear."

I rub my knees and try not to cry.

"Are you alright?" He asks.

"Yes, I'm alright," I tell him.

"Are you sure?" He asks, his eyes burning holes into my knees.

The questions and the rescuing is too much and I snap.

"I'm not weak!" I scream and wince from the jolt of getting angry.

"I never called you weak," John says, in a quiet voice.

The light changes and he makes the turn back down 40, the other direction.

"If you were weak, Ronnie, you wouldn't be able to do everything that you have done," he tells me. "Besides, if you were one of those women that play the abuse card just to get rescued and you go running back, I wouldn't be sitting here right now."

It doesn't take long to go back down the stretch of 40 that lay between the light at 213 and the entrance to the Manor and he's at the light in an instant. There, before turning, as we sit at another red light, he tells me something.

"My second ex-wife roped me in like that," he says. "She was being beat every day and bad, in and out of the fucking hospital. So, I step in and I do the whole rescue thing and I marry her, only to come home one night and find her throwing a party with the abusive ex and all his buddies and they're all taking turns and they're all paying her. She thrived on attention and games, two drugs you will never find a rehab for."

I turn and look at him.

"So, when you say that you're different than you were in high school," he tells me, "Believe me when I say that I am too and I really hated high school."

I laugh, and admit, "I did too, God did I ever."

"High School is like teenage hell, isn't it?" John asks, sarcastically.

"Yeah," I tell him, admitting too, "And, sadly that was only a part of my hell then."

"I know," he whispers, "I know what happened to you. Your store manager bragged about what he had done to everyone. Everyone in town knows what he did to you. And, no one did anything about it."

"How could they?" I ask, adding, "I stayed."

For, even as I had consented and was forced, I was convinced afterwards that this was the way life was to be and I was powerless to change it. So, I had to live with it or else. So, I had stayed as an employee and a sex slave for some months afterwards. Listening to his nonsense for far longer than the human mind can endure.

John turns to me and says, quietly, "Right."

"Enough said," I tell him.

He turns at the light and drops me off at the corner, just before my neighborhood.

Just as I am about to walk away, he leans over the seat and asks, "Are you sure you can make it home because I will lead you to that fucking door and threaten him to say anything."

I smile a little and tell him, "I'm alright, I have to be, because I have work tomorrow."

"I'll see you then," he tells me, adding, "And, I swear I won't walk away again."

"Thank you," I tell him.

He nods, turns the car around and slowly drives away, watching me, I know it, in his rear view mirror. I see no sight of Billy and manage to get the boys from the bus stop and home, with snacks and our afterschool normal activity. I have, what I believe is to be, a quiet night with Billy working all night. So, dinner comes quietly and dishes, showers and nighttime and still no Billy. Just when I'm sure that he will not be home tonight, I take a shower and then slip into a steaming hot bath, hoping to ease the ache in my knees. There, I relish the heat and the muscles relaxing and I'm sure I will be able to sleep without any nonsense.

And, then, just then, the front door opens.

I can hear him walking through the house and unlocking the bathroom door.

And, there he is, ready to torment, because he probably can't find her.

Again.

In the bathroom, I brace for anything, sitting up in the tub, ready to hear nonsense of all kinds. He stomps in, takes a piss, and starts complaining.

"This is what you do with your time now?" Billy asks. "Right, working now and this is what you do with it, like you're something special. Must be nice to get a job where you're fucking the boss. And, then, to lay around in a tub whenever you feel like it."

In defensive mode, I nearly protested that I wasn't fucking Mike or anyone else for that matter and I hadn't sat in this tub in months. But, having had done this so long, I've come to realize that sometimes staying silent is the only thing you can do to survive to the next phase of it all. He keeps bitching that the floor needs to be swept and his room, that's right, his room needs to be cleaned, like he's living in a motel, not paying rent and expecting housekeeping to appear out of nowhere.

Then, he says, "Get out here, we need to talk."

When the bathroom door shuts behind him, I get out of the tub, dry off, empty the water and get dressed. I walk out into the living room and around the corner to the dining room where he is sitting at the dining room table just fit to be tied. He's beside himself and can't sit still that's how pissed off he is and I can't figure out, this is how slow or dumb one that I am, what he would be pissed off at. He has a wife that, despite everything he's done, is not only still with him, but, still willing to put up with his shit, and still remaining loyal and faithful, despite the fact that she has someone willing to give her a good time, in the least, even if for a moment or two until he realizes what he has. He has three beautiful boys that idolize him, God help me that they don't follow in his footsteps. And, a girlfriend on the side that, apparently, his words not mine, is tight and petite and worth the price, a cheap price he has bragged that he gets it for, worth fucking all day and every day that he can and then some.

"So, what's the problem?" I ask, out of patience with him and just so fucking annoyed by this point.

"Well, you apparently have a life of your own now," Billy says, complaining.

"And?" I ask.

"I would like to get fucked tonight and I can't find her," he tells me.

I laugh. I do. I fucking laugh and I can't help myself.

"I'm glad you think it's funny," he says.

"Fine," I say, still laughing, "Did you want me to go track that tight ass pussy down for you? Since I'm her mommy and you need it so bad that you have the balls to complain to me that you can't get fucked? Really?"

"Yeah, that about sums it up," he says.

"Right," I tell him.

"Well, I figured since you're getting fucked now," he has the nerve to say, "I should too."

"I'm not getting fucked," I tell him, against my better judgment, "I'm working."

"Right," he says. "And, you just have all these men willing to defend you because they like your personality so much that that's what they do."

"Well," I tell him, "There are some men in this town that actually appreciate women that they don't have to pay for their attention."

He laughs. "That's cute, real cute."

"Don't be pissed," I tell him, "That I can get it for free and choose not to and you have to hunt her down and pay her to fuck you. I have fucked you. I can see why you need to pay."

He picks up a glass and throws it at the wall. The glass shatters everywhere and the illness starts. I'm yanked off the ground, immediately. Teetering on the edge of a cliff, looking down into nothing. No safety. No one there to catch me.

"I need this and you can't be happy for me," he actually has the nerve to say.

"I'm supposed to be happy," I tell him, "Because you won't fuck me, I'm not worth fucking, I'm too loose, you don't feel anything, aw, I hurt your back, and what else was there? Oh, that's right, you just not feeling it anymore. But, I'm supposed to be happy. Like my shit don't work no more, that's how you're coming across."

He looks at me stunned. My hands are shaking and unlike all the other times before, I'm still running my mouth. This time, the illness may have intervened but the anger at his audacity has taken a front seat to the teetering.

"But, aw, let's be happy for you, shall we?" I continue. "Let's be happy for you and your tight ass pussy prostitute junkie who is now walking the streets looking for her fix and not worried about your dumb fat ass looking to get fucked. Pity. Yeah, I feel sorry for you. Because I'm not the one fucked in the head, you are. There's something seriously wrong with you. There is. And, honestly, it's not like you're well hung. Can she even find it in the dark? I mean, no wonder she's so fucking tight. She's been riding the tiny dick husbands in this town who go home and bitch their wives out for being so blown out when their pussies have stretched around the tiny dicks. I have an option for you. I do. Blow your fucking dick up, get over these complaints, or go and fuck her and live in her fucking tent with her."

His phone goes off at this exact moment. A text message. He turns on his phone, smiles to himself and shakes his head. He looks over at the time and curses.

"A half a fucking hour, which means it's going to be another fucking hour from now," he says, more to himself than to me. And, then, he turns to me, dials 9-1-1 and proceeds to say, in the process of having it ring that his wife is losing her mind and needs to be admitted to the hospital to the fourth floor and can they come get her?

"What do you want me to do?" I ask him.

He tells 9-1-1 that he will call back and let him see what he can do and looks at me and mouths that I am to perform oral sex on him while he waits. Tears well up in my eyes. It's either I do what he wants or I lose everything. I nod. The operator tells him to call back if there is any further problems and he gets off the phone.

An hour later, he's going to the bathroom and I check his phone, sick to my stomach and wanting to run away. He hadn't even made a fucking call. The whole thing was a fucking game. Another game in this marriage, another game in my life. He leaves the house and says, on his way out:

"Nice doing business with you, at least she's worth paying."

And, he's gone and I'm in a corner, screaming and crying.

It's a little after 11 pm, and I find my phone, pulling myself out of my fit, and hold onto for dear life. I pace the floor. I have to make a decision quick, because it won't take Billy long once he gets to her, and I have to decide to call the store or not. I'm tempted to get John's number. Then, I think. No, I decide. I'm so disgusted with myself and so disgusting that I just can't stomach the thought of being near him right now, let alone talk to him. John knows I'm married and he knows what kind of marriage it is, but, suddenly I am dirty and unclean all over again.

Just like in high school.

I put the phone down and share the couch with my oldest, head to feet. I lay facing the back of the couch and pray for sleep. Billy never climaxed, he just made me go through the motions while he criticized and cracked jokes, told me of his impending encounter and made me feel like shit for an hour. I lay there and beg God to hear me.

Please, listen, I beg.

And, then, I pray that Billy never reaches his sexual destination that night. I pray he doesn't find her. That she just vanishes again. And, he can't get his. That's when I get a text.

Here.

It's Billy and my code for when he has her with him and they are about to have sex. So, all my prayers for naught. I close my eyes and count through the time, expecting the next text. A full ten minutes later, it arrives.

Done.

Ten minutes. A whole ten minutes. I cry a little more, think of John. And, then, I make a decision and swear to myself to be sure to keep it by the morning light.

When morning comes, the same decision is there. It's risky, but, it's still there.

I get the boys ready for school, straighten the house a little, and take them to the bus stop. I hug them extra hard that morning and kiss them each on the head before telling them how much I love them and to have a good day at school. And, when the bus pulls away, with them safely inside, I walk to work. Once there, after rehearsing the speech I will give Mike once I arrive, I give him the speech about having to go and take care of something.

He allows me to go, no questions asked.

I promise I will return and leave, saying nothing to John as I pass him.

Chapter 6

Ending

Well that was quick.

And easy.

Nothing like you, let me tell you.

       -there is a reason why my back is toward you

Another forty dollars well spent.

But she's just so fucking unpredictable.

I mean I need to be able to count on her.

       -no one can count on you

I just wish I didn't have to pay her.

       -she's worth the money, though, right?

       -isn't that what you said?

But, that's okay, you're still pissed at me.

I'm the one that's pissed at you.

After all the years of having to deal with pain because of my back.

Now, I can have sex without pain.

She's smaller than you.

It's easier.

                    -right, after all of these years

You should be happy for me.

Isn't that how you feel when you love someone?

  -when you love someone you hurt yourself before hurting them

Well, anyway, the deed is done one more time.

I'm going to have to wait for a few more days to go again, though.

She's so fucking expensive.

Forty dollars for her dope.

And, then, I had to buy her cigarettes.

And a soda and a fucking cookie.

               -but she's worth the money, right?

               -isn't that what you said?

               -that she's worth the money

                    -unlike me

If you lose like eighty pounds, we'd be good.

I'm not saying, I wouldn't want to fuck her.

Hell, I would probably look at big women then online.

You always want what you don't have.

-you don't have me

-does that mean I'm suddenly wanted now

-I weigh less than I did when we first met

-and I've had three kids

-real women don't weigh 95 pounds

-that's what's called the heroin diet, no thank you

Well, I need a shower.

You going to get my clothes for me?

I guess I'll be getting them myself, then.

Babe, everything is just like it was between us.

Nothing has changed.

-right

-and wrong

Do you hear me?

Nothing has changed between us.

We are still together.

We are still one happy family.

Nothing has changed.

-you're wrong

-I have

-I have changed

Chapter 7

The walking girl

I leave the restaurant, backpack still slung over my shoulder and cross 40, toward the cluster of competing fast food restaurants. I weave in and out of traffic and find footing in the grass that outlines the McDonald's parking lot and head down Bridge Street, which is 213 heading in the opposite direction from Chesapeake City. I'm heading toward town and need to get there quick and back again.

And, preferably, alone.

But, as soon as I reach the entranceway of McDonald's I hear a voice behind me.

"You know, if this mission is that important," he begins, "Than, you may need a bodyguard to complete it."

I stop, turn on my heels and face him.

"John," I say.

"Yes?" He asks, innocently.

"That's clever," I tell him. "Clever, but, not going to work."

"I don't like you out here alone," he admits. The sound of his footsteps have stopped and I've managed to walk several feet further away from him by now. I turn to him again.

"You're the only one that worries about me," I admit to him. "So, maybe, you should think that since no one else is worrying, that you shouldn't either."

I'm still reeling from the night before and just feel so disgusting.

He follows at a distance and calls to me, as I cross the double entrance to the mall, "So, what happened last night? You okay?"

"Yeah, I'm fine," I lie.

"Right, and why do I get the feeling that you're lying to me right now?" He asks.

"That's because I am," I say to myself.

"What was that?" He asks.

"Nothing," I tell him, walking slightly faster now.

"You know," he continues, as I cross yet another entrance to a tiny strip mall lining either side of Bridge Street, "I'm not stalking you or anything."

"I know you're not," I tell him.

"Then, tell me what I'm doing," he says.

I stop, turn to face him, wait for him to get closer and stop, then, say, "You're trying to rescue me. I don't need rescuing. I don't. I've been telling you that I'm not like those other women looking for attention. I, unlike them, know that I don't deserve it. I need to remove a problem. And, maybe, I keep thinking, that the only problem here is me."

When I turn to walk away, he says, "I've met female problems and believe me there's many of them. They walk around, some of them looking damn good, makeup and high heels and the biggest pieces of shit known to man. They should come with a warning label."

And, I don't look good, once again, my mind goes there. With no makeup, sneakers, dark hair with streaks of gray pulled back in a lazy ponytail, and heavier than I should be for my height, not disgustingly obese, and not tiny and perfect. Yeah, I'm no prize.

I've stopped even looking in the mirror.

I can't move my feet, standing there, waiting for the other shoe to drop from the other person that I trust right now and just feel so disgusting that I'm trying my damnedest to push away. Instead, he says something sweet without meaning to and without sounding like he is. I don't know how he did it.

But, he says, "You, on the other hand, were meant for a different time, born in the wrong decade I think. No warning label needed."

I can't breathe and not for the wrong reasons, not for any anxiety issues or teetering episodes. I just can't breathe. Tears find their way to my eyes and I tell myself that I have to make this impending decision because my boys need me and if I stay in that house, watching and watching like this imprisoned witness in this sick game, I'll go crazy and they won't have me anymore. I have to fight through this for them.

And, this is a gift I don't deserve, words I had been craving and words that shouldn't be mine. They belong to the beautiful ones, not me, not for someone that's just stuck and can't find her way out of the dark. Those words belong to the innocent. My innocence has long been stolen and kept captive in a sick and twisted mind, played with when he was bored, and lingered over when he was attempting to get his rock soft in the dark.

"Ronnie?" He asks.

I swallow hard and still stand, frozen.

"Yeah?" I ask.

"You okay?" He asks.

"Yeah," I tell him, not knowing how to explain that I just can't do this, any of it.

"Ronnie, look," John tells me, taking a deep breath, "Before and beyond anything else that happens between us and God I hope we have the opportunity and the ability to see what can happen between us, you're a friend. One of the few friends that I have right now and I personally don't let friends face unbearable things alone. I tend to protect them."

I nod and say, "And you say I was born in the wrong decade."

I take a few steps forward, to continue walking, able to feel my legs and to breathe, finally, and I look back to see that he's following. John is standing there, looking at me, waiting for some sign if he can follow or not, refusing to push the bounds of what I will allow. I sigh and shake my head and motion for him to follow.

"I need the moral support anyway," I tell him, once again lying to him and to myself.

He laughs and starts walking, trying to catch up to me, and looking like a little kid that's just been told that they can follow mommy. The thought of that image makes me laugh and I can't stop the smile.

We walk side by side for some time, down Bridge Street and turning right onto Main Street, passing the Post Office and the gathering of the homeless and drug addicts looking like zombies searching for their next high. Without him there I would have been unprotected and exposed because the majority of the homeless that gathering in large groups on Main Street are men, standing around 10 deep and some out of their minds. I pass with the courage of my new bodyguard and head down Main Street, crossing Bow Street and passing empty store fronts and tattoo shops, wedding shops and bail bondsman. I pass the Christmas Shoppe and a few jewelry stores, and at the Bagel shop, I cross over, with John still in step with me, to the old Courthouse. Out front, we smoke, ignore even more homeless clusters gathered, and shoo away the random cigarette leeches that ask anyone smoking for a cigarette.

I can't look at him, while smoking that one cigarette. All I keep doing is rehearsing in my head what my speech will be when I go inside. I have just enough money on me to do what I need to do and for a pack of cigarettes later and I realize that I haven't thought about what I want or how to ask and the fact that my price has always been too low. I even have evidence on me that I need and I decide to ask for money, not of John, but on the paperwork that hopefully will be filed today.

When I'm done, I smoke the cigarette to the butt, I throw it down and tell him, "Wait here, I'll be back."

He nods and looks around, smoking, even turning his back to me as though not to see where I'm going or what I will be doing. I walk pass the giant Elk statue outside, what a waste of money that was, giant Elks dressed up all over the center of town like the Elkton government was cracking a joke that no one really understood the punch line to. Ignoring the one side entrance, I walk around the back of that rotunda, to where I'm directed through the metal detector and just before walking inside, I hold onto the rail and think.

That's when a memory teases the corner of my mind.

Billy and I are sitting out front in the Broncho we had when we first got together. Our oldest is in the back, just two months old and sitting in his car seat, unaware of where we've taken him. I'm dressed up, kind of, and Billy has on a shirt and a tie and jeans. I can't get out of the truck, as my family is filing out of their vehicles and heading inside. Billy opens the driver side door and turns to me.

"What are you doing?" He asks.

"I can't do it," I tell him.

"What?" He asks, shutting the driver side door again. "After all of the hard time you've given me about me doing this again, you now can't do it."

"Me giving you a hard time?" I ask, angry.

"You know what I mean," he says.

"No, I don't," I tell him.

"But, you can't do it?" He asks.

"I can't," I tell him.

"Why?" He asks, impatient.

"Because I watched my parents get divorced, and I don't remember them ever married," I try to explain. "I swore to myself that if I was ever to do this that this would be the only time I do it."

"We actually have to do it first," he says.

"Smartass," I tell Billy.

"Let's go," he says and I obey, out of the truck, Billy carrying our two month old and into the courthouse, where we laugh through the marriage vows and become husband and wife.

And, now, standing there at the same fucking entrance where it began, I can't go in to end it all. I can't do it. I had rehearsed in my head every single little thing that I was going to do and say and now I can't. I just can't.

I pace.

Say to myself, "I can't do it, after every fucking thing you've done, I can't fucking do it. Ten fucking years is too long to throw away, isn't it?"

"Would it help if you just have an affair?" John asks. He's followed me anyway.

I turn to him and say, "No," then, I think about it and add, "Thank you for the offer. That was an offer, right?"

He laughs and tells me, "Absolutely."

"Wow, I've never had that offer before," I admit and then laugh to myself for a moment. That's when the inner tug of war picks up again.

"Maybe it will help to talk about it," he suggests.

"Yeah," I tell him.

And, when I volunteer no information, he asks, "What happened last night to bring this on? If you don't mind me asking because right now I don't know what to ask and how to act. I'm not pushing you to do this, this is between you and him and if you stay with him, we are friends and will remain friends, whatever kind of friend you need. I'm here."

"I know," I tell him, "and, thank you."

"You keep doing that," he says.

"What?" I ask.

"Thanking me," he tells me. "Why do you keep thanking me?"

"Because I'm grateful," I tell him. "It's felt like I've been living in the dark. When I decided to stay and not leave when I found out about her, I lost everyone. Everyone. And, I'm just grateful that you're here. Even if you were to say nothing, you're still here. Thank you."

"So what happened last night?" He presses.

I take a breath and blurt out, "He met up with her, but, because of the insult I gave him, telling him off when he was bitching that he couldn't find her, I had to clean up a broken glass that he threw against the wall, which I didn't clean up until this morning, and I had to blow him for an hour, without him getting his in order to save that rush for her. And, then, he leaves after the hour, nice and pumped up and fucks her, all of ten minutes in and out and comes back bragging about it, telling me that nothing's changed but that she's so much better."

"My God how fucking stupid is he?" He asks the one rhetorical question I've been asking myself for months.

"Right," I reply, still not having the answer to that question and no longer able to even come back with a witty reply once it's asked again, which I guess is why the question is rhetorical.

"I thought he was abusive," he continues, "But, now I just think he's fucking crazy."

I nod.

"And, you know," he goes on, "There's two different kinds of crazy, well more than that, but, in this case two different kinds: one of holding onto a racing car as its speeding away and running into traffic during rush hour. You, my dear, is holding onto the car, while that fucker is just running into traffic crazy."

This makes me laugh.

I tell him, "I do enjoy talking to you."

With a sweet, boyish grin, making his blue eyes dance, he says, "I do aim to please."

I laugh again and say, sarcastically, "In more ways than one, I imagine."

"Oh you know it," he says, laughing, adding, "You sure you don't want to do that affair thing?"

I laugh again and tell him, "No."

"Wow, what a rejection," he says, still laughing.

"Not a rejection," I tell him, adding, "I just don't think I can live with the look of disappointment on your face afterwards."

He laughs again and says, more to himself than to me, "Oh, I have so much work to do, Ronnie. So much work to do, my God. What a stupid, crazy traffic playing fucker you are married to."

"Right," I tell him.

We both laugh.

"I've called him many, many names, believe me," I tell him, adding, "But, right now, I don't know, I can't do this. I can't live in that house with the way things are going, but, I can't leave him either. I just can't."

"Then, don't do it, then," he tells me. "It has to be your decision. Just like you said, I'm not here to rescue you. All I really want is to spend time with you, whatever time you have to give. I'm not trying to gain anything back, I just want a little time."

I look at him, confused.

"Look," he goes on, "Everything went by so fast, like we missed the introductions and the flirting and the conversation and then there was nothing else, like we were dropped in the middle of something fantastic and missed the beginnings and all the boring stuff throughout the middle. And, then, we never even got to see if there was an end or not, or if we sit on the front porch getting old together."

"No one really does that," I correct, knowing that he's right.

"Let's break the mold a little bit, then," he suggests, "And, find a little quiet together, whenever you can give me a slice of time, a few minutes, anything."

"Why?" I ask.

"I thought I answered that," John says.

"No," I tell him, "Why me? Why not someone else?"

"Better looking?" He asks, angry. I nod, he says, "Please don't say to me again."

"Why?" I ask.

"You ask that a lot," he says.

"Yeah, enough said," I say to myself and stare at the courthouse for a few more moments.

I can't bring myself to do it. So, I walk away, without saying a word and John follows. Back on Main Street, we cross Bow Street again and as we're crossing, he's shaking his head.

"I know there's a lot of homeless that kind of wander the town now and stand around during the day," I tell him, adding, "Now, if you lose your house, you get a tent from Social Services. There's a waiting list for fucking tents."

I sigh and he laughs.

"I wasn't thinking that," he admits as we pass the art studio on Main Street.

"What were you thinking then?" I ask.

"That this would have been quicker in a car," he tells me.

I stop, he steps past me several steps before I say, "Really? A car? You're in Elkton now, boy, us Elkton folk walk everywhere."

He turns back to look at me, one eyebrow tipped and several of the homeless groupings let out a roar of laughter, repeating what I had just said.

"Now she's got jokes," he says, before turning and walking away.

I laugh too and wave at the groups, thankful I am not alone, even in daytime.

We get to the light at Main Street and Bridge Street and make a left, down the sloped parking lot and past even more clusters of homeless, just hanging around. I'm thankful it's daytime, by night we'd be passing the streetwalkers and I'd most likely run into her hanging out somewhere up here, looking to get paid in order to get high again. That's when a knot forms in my stomach and I second guess my decision.

For the rest of the time during the walk up Bridge Street to the Mall and across 40 to Mike's restaurant, we say little to nothing. He leads and I find comfort in walking in his shadow. It's peaceful there, a quiet contentment. It helps, seeing that my mind is now playing over the details of Billy's extracurricular activities and her and all that she must mean to him. I have told myself that just watch from a distance, that the whole thing between Billy and his whore will just kind of fizzle away, but, there's only so much that someone can actually watch without completely losing it.

And, honestly, I'm tired of being a witness to insanity.

As we cross 40, he reaches back and takes my hand, traffic is relentless, and he leads me across safely. It's a small gesture, but, it erases the bad from my mind in an instant. I'm able to refocus and find safe footing in my direction for the day. Back at Mike's, he pauses out front, gives me one of his cigarettes, and as we smoke we have another chance to talk.

"So, a little time?" He asks.

I look away.

He sighs and says, "I'm not going to get that, am I?"

I swallow hard and tell him, "I need a little time in order to be able to give you a little time."

He thinks for a moment and takes a drag off his cigarette and says, "You can have however much time you need."

His words say that, he has spoken that sentiment, but, his face is disappointed and I'm sure that I've just managed to push a good thing right out the door again. I go back to work and see little of John for the rest of the day and then he's just gone again.

I walk home after work, get the boys from the bus stop after school, and walk them home. There, after giving them their snacks and hearing about their day, Billy and I set down and talk. We make a deal. And, I agree to it, working on us, but, more than that, changes.

Chapter 8

Deals

-can we work on us?

Sure, what's on the table?

-what do you want on the table?

Well, you quit your job.

-and what do you do?

Give more time to you.

-okay

And, no mention of divorce.

-deal

You need to be on medication, though.

You're really just losing it and you need medicine.

-and how are we going to help that situation?

By you going on meds.

-so there's nothing you can do to help that?

I've agreed to spend time with you.

And, nothing has changed though.

-what do you mean?

I still need to have sex and I can't have sex with you.

-can't or won't

I need to have pain free sex and I can't do it with you.

-I'll lose weight

Eighty pounds is a lot of weight.

-can you live with fifty pounds?

How long is that going to take you?

Because you know I'm running out of money.

-no one told you to go and pay for sex, did they

You gave me no choice.

And, look, we're talking about working on us and you turn it into an argument.

-right, what do you want me to do?

Lose weight, no divorce, work on us, and sleep in the bed with me.

-give me a reason to

I love you, babe.

I do. Nothing has changed between us.

-I have

Well, you still have a long way to go in that change, don't you?

-and you want?

I don't want to hurt you.

I know you don't believe it.

But, this was never about you or hurting you.

-but you did and you made it about me

How did I?

-by every reason being my fault

What do you want me to do?

Not see her?

-yes

Fine I won't see her then.

Two days later, life is unbearable and he can't stand any of us. He hates me and the boys and can't stop yelling and moping and throwing shit around. I go to him in his room. I'm still not sleeping in there.

-you can have her

-I'll do whatever you want me to do

Thank you, babe.

I love you, I do.

Nothing has changed.

-everything has changed

How can you say that?

-don't you see it?

-everything has changed

-why am I even fighting when you're not wanting us

I do.

I do want us.

Let me do what I have to do and get it out of my system.

But, nothing has changed.

It's just that there isn't any sex between us.

You take care of me and lose weight, don't work and we'll work
on us.

-right

Sounds good, right?

I mean, it's a lot better than a mental institution, right?

Because, right now, you need one.

-yeah, I'm the one that needs one

So, do we have a deal then?

-whatever you want

Chapter 9

The smaller girl

The smaller girl should be congratulated. She should be applauded and rewarded for her efforts. The smaller girl, now at that place where she's not quite there where she's going and yet so far from where she's come, sitting on the side of the road between both destinations and unsure of which way to go. This would be the time to encourage the smaller girl to keep going forward.

Instead, criticism abounds.

She is nothing. She is lazy, unmotivated, and wasting her energy. She is unfocused and at the cause of all of his needs. She never takes care of him, ignores his hardened medical condition as it arises, and busies herself with useless activities. She bitches and complains and does nothing constructive.

So the smaller girl sits and waits and waits some more. For what is she waiting for? She doesn't even know. But, she's smaller and a little more confident. A little.

And, I mention this last lightly.

I lost twenty five pounds in that first month when I first found out about Billy and his whore. And, then, after the deal, was another 10 pounds in that month that followed. And, now another five, making a total of 40 pounds lost since he started paying her for sex. I walk several hours a day, through the house, of course. I only go to the bus stop and the store, as needed, and he sends me a text when he's at his spot with her and texts me when he's done.

I'm not sleeping again.

I'm still not on any medication and I'm not sleeping in bed with him as of yet. And, the way he's been acting, I don't think that that will ever happen. Where I was far less than any other human on the planet, I'm now even lower. And, if I do sleep in bed with him, it will appear that I'm chasing him, and after all this time, I don't have it in me anymore to chase him or anyone else for that matter. I'm too tired and discouraged and honestly after being married for ten years, why should I have to chase him? Either he wants me or he doesn't. Period. Cut and dry. To lie to myself and have him lie to me is draining.

So, I put my head down and keep pushing forward.

I don't see any hint of John. Then again, how could I? Stuck in the house and being monitored like I was the one cheating and not Billy. And, my list of daily chores continues to grow. I long for the moment at the levies again. I do. Just to feel human and feminine and sexual and wanted. I long for that moment and would do nearly anything right now for it.

Its night and I'm sitting at the dining room table, unable to sleep. And, I try to remember all of the little band aids I would use in order to make it through and pass and complete the being a forced witness to his insanity and I think about my own online flirtation. Short lived and leaving only emptiness behind.

But, there had been this voice, or rather words that had helped me at one point.

So, I go back into the old email and search, desperately, for the one I had been flirting with. And, it wasn't even flirting, it was leaning on that person. I had been on this sex website years ago, when the communication was free, and I had been looking for some validation on my looks after Billy had gone months telling me how unattractive I was. And, there had been this guy I was talking to, all sexual at first, and then, I had sent a picture of myself, at first nude, without a face shot. And, the conversation continued sexually. Then, he asked for a face shot of me, and when I had sent it, the conversation suddenly changed and I never fully understood why. It's just that it became, from then on, a leaning on thing.

At the time, I had assumed that it was another form of rejection. So, I just accepted that I was unattractive, took off my information from the site and just emailed him and him alone. Because, no matter the rejection, I needed the encouragement. I needed that voice, the words in the dark places of my life. And, I never went back to a sex site again, sure that I was so unattractive that I'd be rejected again and again and again.

So, for years, off and on, I had leaned on him, repeatedly, and he had always been there. Now, with the kids asleep and the television on, in order to keep them asleep, I search for the email and find it.

I fight the guilt, yet again, like I always had to do, and scribble a rambling email. Before hitting send, I read and reread it again.

It's been awhile, but, I need you. I'm stuck. Locked away and I've asked for this.

I have. I've asked for this pain. But, I need to connect with you again.

If you haven't completely given up on me, please read this and respond.

I glance once more at the boys sleeping and hit send. Moments later, I get a response.

I've been waiting for you, honey. Waiting. It's been too long.

Don't do that to me again. I've been worried and searching everywhere.

Just to see you. Just to know that you're okay.

I read the email and pause.

I've never seen him and I've spoken to him for years, off and on, leaning on him when the madness became too maddening and I was in the same place I am now. Lost and lonely, betrayed and seeking just a kind word and a way of venting everything that Billy would never listen to. There were moments over the years that I wished I could meet the one I was emailing. Because Billy wouldn't allow me to even cry. He would cause the pain and get angry whenever the tears came. I don't know why I didn't see it then, but, it was like being in high school and standing out back of the store where I worked and my rapist yelling at me to stop my fucking crying. No one wants to see your tears. No one wants to hear you cry.

And, now, I'm confused.

When did my email companion ever see me?

I write another email.

I'm sorry. But, when did you ever see me?

I hit send and wait. For long moments, there is nothing. And, then, I get a response.

Oh, honey, I have so much to tell you.

I've been waiting, but, you have nothing to be sorry about.

I knew that if it went bad, this is what you would do.

I've been sitting here, refreshing my email, constantly.

I read and reread the response. I look around, not sure of what to do. Then, I write my own response and hit send.

Who is this?

This response was quicker.

In order to answer this question, I will send you this.

Your voice aids in leveling me again, the good among the dark,

I have little to give you, but, the shattered pieces of my heart.

I read the response and tears well up in my eyes, blinding the screen and its words from my grasp. I wipe the tears away and reread it again and again and again. The two lines scrawled on the piece of paper in order to pull him to safety dance now in front of my eyes. I collapse on my laptop and rock back and forth.

John hadn't just showed up out of nowhere, wanting something back that he thought he had missed in high school. He had been here, all along, holding onto me in his times of need and there for me in mine. Through both of his divorces and through unspoken damaging disappointments, he had emailed me and I had encouraged him along the way, secretly. To only push him away, once the guilt became too much and followed me around the house like another resident here. And, when Billy's flirtations became too much, when I forced to be a witness to his online games and then to his physical ones, this latest junkie hadn't been the first but had been the only one he had hidden, I had leaned on him through email, knowing only a screen name and nothing more. I had always felt safe in doing so, since he lived at such a distance from me: New York.

And, it had been him all along. It had been John.

And, there had never been a rejection to my looks, he had realized who it was and pulled back, wanting something more. This was more than a sexual encounter to him, not a flat out I'm too ugly and not wanted thing. I cry harder, realizing that I hadn't been rejected all of those years ago, rather I had been held close, protected, and hidden away, not to prevent my eyes from seeing the rest that I shouldn't see, despite all that I was seeing. But, rather hidden away like a gem that was for his eyes only and not for random strangers.

I write another email, frantically, my hands shaking and hit send.

My God it's you. It's you. Why the fuck didn't you tell me?

After several moments, the response comes and I read it and read it again.

Ha ha, when wooing the damsel, one does not tell all of the secrets.

At least, not all at once.

A sweet moment and he has to fuck it up with humor. I shake my head and realize that the response is as sweet as the knowledge that my secret shoulder had been him all along. I laugh, through tears, and want to hunt him down, wrap my arms around his neck as much as I want to throw the damn laptop at him. How the fuck do I get into a position where I want to love someone and hurt them at the same time?

That's when I realize that I've used the word love, even if only in my thoughts.

Love. Something I'm sure I'm incapable of, something I was sure was lost to me forever. When you have to be a witness to someone's rejection of you for so long, you're sure that love will never find you again. When you have to listen to how low you are in their eyes, wanting only to be acceptable in their sight, you're sure that life has this in mind for you and nothing else.

Love.

I didn't think I'd ever know myself to even think the word ever again. And here I am.

I write another email and send.

Is this from some secret book you've read?

You know one of those how to books.

And, how often have you used this book on said damsels?

I laugh to myself, having had decided that I would match humor with humor, and wait for the response. I imagine his aged face crinkling in a delicious smile and those ocean blue eyes sparkling with his laugh. And, then, the response comes.

Good, you can still find humor.

And, no, that handbook is just for you.

God, I've been going crazy without you around.

This is contact with you, but, I'm going to be honest.

But, he never finishes the email, he never finishes his thought. I read the email and reread it and realize that he was using humor to try to refocus me, but, the unfinished email bothers me. I wait for long moments and nothing comes.

I write another email and send.

What do you want to be honest about?

That you don't really want me either?

I remember your reaction to my nude pictures.

What do you want to be honest about?

Because, trust me, after everything I've had to see, I can take it.

Whatever it is, I can take it.

The answer takes longer. I figured that with my email, I would test my theory, still unsure of myself after the initial rejection years before. And, after losing all of this weight, all I see is all of the weight I still have to lose and nothing more.

No, baby, I never rejected you.

If you remember, I asked you to not send any pictures to anyone else.

I still have those. Trust me, they've been used, by me.

Many times (face red) in my private moments.

I've missed you, I mean that.

I cry and hate the fact that I'm now crying happy tears. Old teachings are hard to break, I guess. Billy never liked those tears either. When I would cry happy tears over the big moments in our life together, he'd bitch for days afterwards, until I was hardened even against those tears.

And the thought that I am attracted enough to provide fodder for another man's, specifically John's, fantasy, even heavier than I am now, makes me feel better. Someplace inside that I hadn't known in years begins to untighten and unwound itself. There's this spark of something and I'm not sure of what it is.

I write another email and send.

Then, what do you want to tell me?

I wait for the response. Like the one before, it takes a long time, and then it arrives.

I want to hold you again.

Don't stop talking to me again or push me away.

Don't let guilt talk you out of talking to me.

I'm just telling you that I want to hold you again.

I do. And, honestly, much more than that.

I cry and scribble the next response and hit send.

I won't.

Tell me what more you want to do.

I wait and his response comes quick. One simple question.

What has he done to you?

I read the response and don't know quite of how to reply.

So, I stare at the page for long moments and can only find one answer to the question.

Nothing and everything.

As I hit send, I'm unsure if he'll understand the code and the answer and will get what I'm alluding to at all, if he even understands what I've just sent. I have this tremendous fear that he'll simply stare at the email, and nothing more.

Instead, he responds:

So, he's hurting you and ignoring you.

He's making you watch him leave to go to her.

And, you are what? The servant in the house.

With hand over my mouth, the surge of tears pushing through, I nod at the computer screen. I take a moment, eyes closed against the pain, and compose myself. I write another email and hit send.

I'm not one of those women.

A few moments later, the response comes.

Stop comparing yourself.

You are not one of those women.

Nor will you ever be one of them.

Be strong. I'm here. If you can get through tonight, work toward that.

Don't take so much of spaces of time.

Little by little. When you're ready to go, you have somewhere to go.

Where is he now?

I read the email, blurred as the message is, and write my response and hit send.

Where do you think?

I wait and he is quicker with this one.

Looking for her or with her?

I answer.

With her at a motel.

Because, apparently, there are things he wants to do that he can't.

At least not in a vehicle.

It is some time before he answers and when he does I can hear the fury in his thoughts, even if I'm only reading his words.

My God, Ronnie, I'm going to fucking kill him.

He's fucking crazy. What the fuck?

I answer, fighting the urge to defend the fact that Billy did have the nerve to ask me to my face if he could do the motel room thing. But, he hadn't been asking his wife. No, it was as though he had been asking his mother. It was that conversation, two days ago, that I realized that I had never truly been married. I had adopted a child and nothing more. There had been no protection, no covering, no love between us, only the words and a shared experience of children and the need to survive.

I can't stand myself. The skin I'm in is too close, too tight, too suffocating. I want to run and I can't think straight. My boys need me, here and now, to continue lying to them that everything is alright and nothing bad is happening to them or to me. I want to run and stay here, only because of them. I'm in a wilderness and I can't see, it's dark and I'm without vision, even to the next moment.

I don't like this feeling. I'm flying blind and teetering far too high.

I write a response and hit send.

I could give you the excuse, but, there is none.

Not for this.

The only thing I can say is that this is my fault.

I take full responsibility for allowing this to continue.

I am nothing.

I am on pause, waiting to hear what will happen now.

Please, don't leave.

The response that comes I hold onto through the next few days. It is fast coming and powerful in its revelation to me. That's why I hold onto as though I will never see John's face again.

It isn't your fault.

You are the only one that doesn't have any blame in this.

If anything, you are in need.

And, I can promise you everything and give you less than what I've promised.

Instead, I will say, that I can try.

He's not even trying anymore, if he ever did at all.

Trying, at least, implies that you want to give and you fail.

Not trying is refusing to give anything.

I can and will try.

Just then, as I read and reread the email, Billy comes thundering in, pissed off at the world and at her and I'm about to hear every single detail. Once again, a forced witness.

Chapter 10

Failures

I swear to fucking God I've wasted money on that bitch.

-what happened now?

I give her fucking money, pay for the motel room, and nothing.

-oh, you mean, you didn't get yours?

-how nice

-is that the complaint we're working with?

She disappears, to get her shit, and then comes back and complains about soda.

I give her more money and she's at the store next door.

She comes back with cigarettes and soda.

-aw, your girlfriend has needs

She comes back, and takes an hour on her fucking hair.

And, then, I'm watching television waiting for her.

And, she boots up right there, taking her shit.

-she is a junkie, that's what they do

I don't want to fucking see it.

-and living with her would have been better how?

She then gets undressed and lays in bed, higher than a fucking kite.

-junkie

And, just none responsive.

Nothing.

I'm playing with her, and trust me there's nothing to her body.

-she's nineteen and looks like a little girl

-how arousing for you

I can't even get fucking hard.

So, no, I don't get mine.

What a waste of fucking time.

-I'm so sorry that your junkie didn't come through

-you know with your whole sex thing

-like you're in a porno and the actress didn't make it to work

-right

I've wasted so much fucking money today.

I should have just fucked her in the van again.

Honestly, what the fuck was I thinking?

-you weren't

What am I going to do now?

I mean, I want to do so many things.

And, I just can't do them with you.

-like I'm gargantuan and I can't have sex

-right

Babe, a little advice, what the fuck am I going to do?

-I'm not your mother, dude

-I'm not and the advice train has now stopped

-find another one

-you know all of them on Main Street

-I'm sure that won't be hard

But, I've worked so hard on this one.

Buying her shit and buying her cookies and soda and fucking cigarettes.

What the fuck am I going to do now?

Chapter 11

The broken girl

There's only so much you can break a broken girl before she shatters and is absolutely invisible. There's only so much a broken girl can take before she snaps and becomes a different person altogether. There's only so much that a broken girl can withstand before the weight of it all breaks anything and everything within that is left of her foundation.

Take her, mold her, and train her. The ugly girl, the working girl, the walking girl, the starving girl, and the smaller girl will just deal. She will accept what you give her and make it beautiful and protect it as though it were a gem. Even if you don't treat her as such, she will treat the small amount of attention that you give her in this way. That is nature. And, that is just the way she does things in order to have a happy life. In order to survive.

But, push her, break her, make her witness your insanity, and tell her to let it all go while you continue on going crazy and making her the same, and she will become just numb. Numb to it all. Numb to you and your fantasies. Numb to you and your lies. Numb to all the shit that you throw at her.

Just simply numb.

That's where I was when he sat across from me bitching. Bitching about her not coming through for him and bitching about all the money she now owes him and that he will take it out of her one way or another.

And, the image of yesterday combined with the man that I married into this terrible image that I never thought I would see together and intertwined. And, all at once, I was my abuser's wife, sitting at home, questioning why it had taken him so long to come home after work and hearing the foul mouth excuses in return. I was in her place and I hated it there, about as much as I hated being the one slammed on the floor and taken so violently.

But, I refuse to place myself in that nineteen year old's shoes even for a moment.

Instead, as he's bitching and complaining and brainstorming about how to get his much needed pussy, like mine is suddenly missing, and from him I guess it is, I send a good night email to John.

Thinking of you.

Have to go.

He's back and he's angry.

Apparently, she's not all she's cracked up to be.

Go figure.

I mute my computer, so that I can get the response and not have it bring any attention from Billy. The last thing I need right now is to deal with his nonsense.

The response comes as Billy is talking about the nineteen year old's sister, who is a professional, at the same rate, mind you, but professional in the giving of sex once she's paid.

Aw, the little junkie can't be trusted.

Pity. Most junkies can't be. Doesn't he know this?

Wow, he is stupid, fucking stupid.

Get some sleep.

Lay in my arms tonight.

I'll be holding you.

If you can't sleep, I'm here.

Hide these emails. I want you safe.

I respond as Billy texts the nineteen year old's sister and gets an immediate response.

Will do.

Feel more than I say.

Apparently, the sister is quick and wants to meet tonight. So, he sits there, looks around, counts his money in his head, and is standing like he's going to leave. But, then, he thinks and sends her another message, causing him to sit down again.

I get a response, just before closing the computer.

Love you, too.

Right, I think. I hide the emails in a folder entitled poetry, which Billy would loathe to look inside of, and close the computer. I sit and look across the table at Billy.

With my hands in my lap and a poker face on that I didn't think I was capable of, I ask him, "So, are you going to see her sister, then?"

"What the fuck do you expect me to do?" He asks.

"Is that a yes?" I ask.

He is suddenly irritated, answers, "Yes, I am."

"Right," I say, adding, "So, this is just going to keep going. No matter who it's with, you're just going to keep fucking around with any little pay by sex pussy you can find. Just as long as their tiny and their cheap and you can get to them quick."

This pisses him off and he throws the soda bottle at me. It is half full and whizzes by my head and hits the wall behind me. I'm usually, at this point, breaking down and ready to do whatever needs to be done. But, since the glass shattering, I'm unmoved.

I look back at him and reply, "I guess that's a yes then."

Billy, noticing my lack of reaction, lowers his head and apologizes, saying, "I'm just pissed, that's all. I paid for something and I expect to get it."

Inside I'm wanting the levies and the past before my life veered completely off course.

"I just," he continues, "Feel like I've been taken for a ride and I want my money back or want to get laid tonight, whichever comes first."

Billy thinks for a moment and then says, "Ha, at least I can cross that off my bucket list."

"What is that?" I ask, bored.

"Two things actually," he says, "Sisters and two twenties, since her sister is twenty one. I guess you're wrong then."

"How am I wrong?" I ask, while inside I'm making a list of just how very wrong I've been.

"You said I wasn't wired for two twenties," Billy says. "I guess you're wrong then."

"We'll see," I say, numb all at once.

It's not the fact of forcing me into this conversation as much as the joke that has been told in the midst of it. Telling me that he needs pussy and has paid and when he pays for something he expects to get it. No, that was the least, for I've been watching this so long now, a forced witness to this atrocity. No, it was the joke afterwards.

He leaves and I walk him to the door. There, I tell myself that I'm done. If he goes through this and fucks the sister, he will never see me again, he will never have his family again. I'm done and I won't leave. He will. Even if I don't kick him out, the marriage is over. It was over long ago, if it ever existed at all, and it merely existed on paper.

Fifteen minutes later, I receive the expected text message:

Here.

Twelve minutes after that, the follow up message:

Done.

I go to bed, earphones jammed into my ears and I lose myself in the music of breakups, love lost, and love yearned for. I eventually go to sleep, imagining that I'm lying in John's arms and all is well and right in my world. The sound of the water and the bugs and the peaceful stillness of the levies surrounding us like a comforting blanket.

The next day, I get up, get the boys off to school and clean the house. I avoid Billy as much as I can. But, seeing how small our house is, I can only avoid him so much. When we do run into one another, he brags about the night before.

"Well, she's quieter than her sister," he brags, sitting on the arm of the loveseat.

I try to block him out by cleaning the boys' disgrace of a room. With five garbage bags in hand, I sit at one corner and slowly go through every inch of their things. He is still talking and his voice carries into the bedroom. I can't get away from the conversation.

"Her sister grabs and pulls on my shirt," Billy tells me, referring to the nineteen year old's actions during sex. "While she doesn't grab, doesn't make a sound, gets in and gets the job done. I like her. She knows what she's doing."

I close my eyes against the wave of pain and feel the numb come on just as fast.

He continues, "I didn't have to search for her. She was exactly where she said she would be. I paid her, much cheaper than her sister by the way, and we went and got it done."

I throw trash and some broken toys into the trash bag and notice my hands are shaking.

Billy continues, by saying, this time, he's moved to the couch's arm right by the boys' bedroom, "Even though, I have to admit, that the grabbing on my shirt and the sounds are erotic. It's a huge turn on."

I nod, have to say, I can't help myself, it just comes out, "But, when I do it, I'm told to stop because you want to protect your shirts."

"Well, it's different when you do it," he says, adding, "And, I've never said that to you."

I turn to him, tell him, "You have."

When I turn back and start cleaning again, he says, "Well, not to sound gross or to hurt you or anything, but, you told me to get tested. I use condoms and the last time I was with her," the nineteen year old, "I play around with her pussy when she's sucking him to get him hard, and I went to stick one finger in and I couldn't get it in, so, I really don't think she's what you think she is. She's not fucking around or anything."

"Wow," I say, in order to silence him, "I didn't know that heroin did that to a female."

I place a few more broken toys and random pieces of trash into the bag and refuse to turn around and face him. From behind me, I hear him sigh like he's irritated and he stomps his foot annoyingly.

Billy then says, "You know I'm sharing this with you, because that's what I'm supposed to do. And, this is the way you act and react."

That's it, I've had enough. I throw the bag aside and stand and face him.

"I'm not your friend," I yell at Billy. "I'm not. I'm your fucking wife, you lowlife piece of shit. Honestly, you come in here bragging about fucking your fucking whores like I'm your fucking pal. Who the fuck are you? Seriously, you have something seriously, mentally wrong with you. How am I supposed to fucking react? And, no, you're only sharing this with me now. You don't remember hiding all of this bullshit from me? Or, are you too fucking dead set on them that you've completely forgotten that you're fucking married?"

"I haven't forgotten," Billy says with a smile.

"God, I'm out of here," I tell him, and storm out of the room.

As I pass him, he grabs hold of me and pulls me close to him, grabbing my breast and forcing me to straddle his knee. He pinches my nipples until the pain surges up through my breast. I wince and back away and he pulls me closer again.

"Well," he tells me, "You still give the best blow jobs around. You should be proud of that. Why aren't you proud of that?"

I try to get out of his grasp and can't. I look away ignoring him. He pulls me close to him and bites my neck.

"Stop hurting me," I tell him.

Billy then pinches the under skin of my arm. Pain surges through my arm. And, I tell him to stop.

"But, I love you," he says.

"Then, stop hurting me," I tell him.

He's left bruises before this way and I'm sure this has left its own mark, yet again.

"But, that's how I show you that I love you," Billy tells me.

"You don't love me," I tell him.

"Sure I do," he says, adding, "How can you say that? Babe, I need to do this. Be happy for me. I'm finally getting what I need. I know I've spent a lot of money, but, come on. I need this. Let me have this."

I shake my head and look away.

"And, you were wrong," he tells me.

"About?" I say, wanting to get away.

"I am wired for two twenties," he says and bites my neck again.

I fight to get out of his grasp and can't. Billy pulls me close to him, forces his hands under my shirt and under my bra, pushing the lump of clothes upward, exposing my breast, and bites my nipple. I push him away, using my hands against his face.

"Why do you hurt me?" I scream.

Tears are welling up in my eyes and I fight to get out of his grasp.

Once I'm free, I walk away, telling him over my shoulder, "You're a fucking asshole."

"Oh, what did I do now?" He asks.

I leave the house, grabbing everything I need on the way out, and lighting a cigarette once my feet hit the ground out front. I walk out of the neighborhood, wiping the tears from my eyes and I can still feel the throb of my throat, my arm, and my breast. I rub my breast as I head across 40, toward town, and wonder if all men act this way.

On Main Street, I pass her. I do. I pass her. I roll my eyes and keep walking straight. I try ignoring her, but, it is just too much. Honestly, way too much. I grab my phone and once it's in hand, she takes off away from me, making a beeline toward the Manor.

"Go on to my house, you fucking whore," I say, loud enough for her to hear, and keep walking.

Just then, my phone goes off.

I look down, swipe the screen. It's a text message, from Billy.

I'm sorry, okay?

Just come home.

Rather than answering him back right away, I check my email. And, sure enough John has emailed me, sometime in the early morning.

I open the email.

Thinking of you. Holding you. Loving you.

Once again, I don't know what to do. I'm so used to being ordered around that I now look to Billy for my acceptance. I look to him for decisions, for everything, sitting under a covering full of holes. I look to him for direction. And, now, he's telling me to come home and I don't even feel like I have a home anymore. My home is where my boys are, but, it's their home, not mine.

I sit down on the curb and cry. Covering my head with my hands, it's all I can do. I don't have the courage or the strength to walk away yet. Am I addicted to the pain or to Billy? I have myself to set right. I have to do something to fix me, to fix this. Can I fix this? Was there anything in those ten years that's worth saving now? Did he ever love me at all?

I cry. And, I'm alone. I don't have anyone to lean on, outside of John, and I can't do it. I can't lean on him. The guilt is too much. I'm just as bad as Billy is for allowing this to continue on as long as it has, but, I can't let go. I can't.

I cry for a while and then I just walk.

For hours, I walk, wandering through town and purposely down Main Street, drifting in and out of the cluster of homeless men standing around. Each group make comments and watch me walk pass. I'm alone and lost and not caring what happens to me.

Just as one of the homeless men start following me, a familiar car pulls up, and a voice calls from the driver's side door.

"Get in," he says, adding, "Now, before I have to fight off a gang that wants to do God knows what to you."

I stop and turn toward him.

"John, please," I beg, "Stop saving me. I'm not looking to be saved."

He exhales, the smoke lingers and carries off toward the crowd now gathered and looking elsewhere as though they hadn't been following.

He then says, "Those that need it, don't want it and don't ask for it, ever. Please, for me, I'm not trying to save you, I'm trying to protect you and to stop you from doing something stupid. A friend, remember. Get in, please, Ronnie."

I glance back and realize that I had been careless. And, I lower my head, embarrassed, and I get into the car. There, he runs his hand through my hair and speeds off down Main Street.

"I swear," he tells me, "You're now becoming self-destructive. What the hell am I going to do with you?"

"The same thing the other thing does," I snap, sarcastically.

"What's that?" He asks.

"Hurt me," I tell him and collapse in tears.

Chapter 12

Angry

I'm not going to hurt you.

What did he do?

How did he hurt you?

            -don't worry about it.

        -just drop me off around the corner.

What did he do to you?

          -please, everything is fine

        -just drop me off around the corner

Honey, listen to me.

              -listen to me

              -just drop me off

                -PLEASE

No, I'm not dropping you off.

Listen to me, I'm worried about you.

          -stop worrying about me

        -no one else does and you shouldn't either

-don't you realize that I get what I deserve

No, you don't.

You deserve so much more than this.

What the fuck happened?

-stop asking me questions

-it doesn't matter

-don't you fucking get it?

-it doesn't matter

It does matter.

Tell me what fucking happened?

What did he do to you?

-please

-just drop me off around the corner

I'm not dropping you off.

Not until you tell me what happened.

I want to help you.

I'm here, don't you get that.

I've always been here, let me be here for you.

-everyone is gone

-and you'll be gone, too

-just fucking walk away now

-don't make me wait until I'm comfortable and safe to fucking walk away

I'm not going anywhere.

I'm not leaving you.

What happened?

What did he do to you?

-it doesn't fucking matter

-just drop me off around the corner

-leave me alone and let me deal with it

No, I'm not going to do that.

-what is it with everyone not giving me a fucking choice?

Is this what you want?

-yes

I don't believe you.

I don't believe you.

-why do you even care?

Because I do.

And, I can't change the way that I feel.

I can't help how I feel.

                              -how do you feel?

I love you, Ronnie.

The car stops at a stop sign on Main Street and I get out and walk away.

Saying nothing.

Chapter 13

The happy girl

The happy girl is only happy through a sacrifice of her own. Her will, her standards, her ability to demand more, and even her own peacefulness. She finds happiness in her own sacrifice, for giving happiness to others is expected, but, receiving happiness comes with a price. The price, though, is too steep for some. But, there are the rare few that will take the price and give more than what is expected, even as the happiness doesn't increase with the increased sacrifice. And, sometimes the happiness is far less and still the happy girl will sacrifice more just to be accepted by the only man that she is sure will ever accept her.

And, he's the only man that may never know, or care, just exactly what treasure he has.

That's where I am.

I go home, obediently, and accept his apology. For my efforts, he makes clumsy complaint-filled love to me, well sort of. It starts out this way and ends up with me taking care of him as though it's a medical condition and I'm the nurse on call for the moment.

Well, at least I got a little sex, I tell myself. And, learn, just then, after ten years, of how to hide my anger with the rest of it behind being fake. You know the rest of it: pain, disillusionment, the discouragement, and just this tremendous sadness. All of it I push down into one tight ball of emotions that I hide behind this fake exterior of being the perfect wife and mother, housewife and partner. The house becomes, starting that day, obsessively clean. And, after delivering his clothes to him in the bathroom for his shower and handing him his towel, he is knocked off guard and unsure of what to do or what to say.

I push John out of my head, telling myself that I couldn't afford losing him when he realized what a piece of trash he really had. What a piece of trash he'd have by being with me. I think his realization of it would be more heartbreaking than anything going on in my life right now and worse than anything that has happened thus far. So I convince myself that pushing him away is the best thing that I can do.

So, after catering to Billy all day, taking care of the boys, and when they're asleep, aid in catering to Billy yet again, which causes him to sleep, I then sit down at my computer and send an email to John.

I'm sorry about today. Please forgive me.

But, you deserve better than this, better than me.

I'm sorry. You more mean to me than I'm willing to admit.

But, you need to find someone worth the chase and the fight.

I sit back and wait, hoping that the push in that direction will work.

And, John refuses to be pushed away.

His response is adamant:

Do what you can in order to survive.

But, I'm not walking away from you.

I haven't done it yet and I'm not going to.

There's something about you that you're not seeing.

I see it and I don't want to live without it anymore.

So, try to push me away, I won't go.

I'm not leaving. I'm not going to overwhelm you.

But, you do the survival thing and let me take care of what I have to take care of.

I read it and reread it, hiding it, once again, in my personal folder and sit there thinking.

He deserves so much more than this. He does. A nice girl without baggage. I've always thought of myself the non-baggage girl and I was wrong. This is baggage, all of it. Not the kids, mind you. But, Billy and his nonsense and the damage he has already caused to me and my ability to trust again.

So, fight as I have to not be that girl. I am that girl and I can't stand it.

I try that approach before closing up the email and trying to get some sleep.

I send a response to John:

How much bullshit do you want to carry then?

Because I apparently come with baggage and I hate the extra luggage.

I said I wasn't that person and I guess I am after all.

I'm sorry. I am. I thought I was weight free and I'm not.

I send it and am half tempted to just walk away, not waiting for the response. But, something inside needs a little validation or something and I sit and wait to hear back from him. Either that or I just can't stand arguing with John, of all people, and need the peaceful conclusion to the whole thing, even if it is a goodbye.

A few moments later, the response comes:

You are weight free. It's just that your chains are weighty.

You're chained there, to him, and you will do what you have to do.

I get that and I'm not holding that against you.

Just tell me that you don't want me out of your life.

I read the email and reread it, fighting the tears back.

But, if I'm doing this faking thing to figure out what the fuck to do next, and pushing all of the rest of it aside, I have to be all in or all out. I'm not a half road sort of person, I'm not half in or half out. It has to be all or nothing. So, I compose, in my head, a pushing him away without hurting him speech that I am trying to word just right before sending it in an email, when I hear Billy's phone go off.

It's a text message.

I get up from the computer and walk through the house, to our room, where he is still sleeping. I walk around the bed, still watching him, and pick up his phone. There is a message. It's from her:

Sorry, babe, my phone died.

I'll see you tomorrow night then.

I put the phone down and have this odd feeling come over me. It's a cross between standing naked in front of a room full of strangers and that feeling that you must get when you've been handed an award that is really meant for someone else. I stand there a moment or two. And, I think.

The room is quiet, dark, the smell of sex strong, and his snores the only sound.

I look around and decide that I am worth more than this. It's an odd feeling, some realizations as they come, and I don't know what to do now. Like I've been settling for this when I could have so much more out of life and love and the boys could have more and my happiness now is standing in the room with me, a broken little girl that's been lost all this time.

What the hell do I do?

I leave the room and go back to the computer.

I write one last message that night and hit send.

I want you in my life.

I do. I'm still not there, on sure footing and grounded.

Your voice has stopped the anxiety attacks.

That's all I really know. Is that you have pulled me out of this huge hole.

Time and again and again and again.

But, I'm not wanting to weigh you down because I'm not free.

I do want you in my life.

Please don't go, but, find your own happiness.

Where I can't have any right now, you can, and will.

I wait to see if he responds. And, during my wait, Billy comes stumbling out of the room, to go to the bathroom, and stops right before the door. He turns to me and says:

"So, you're messing with my phone again, are you?"

"I heard your phone go off," I tell him.

"Right," he says, "And, you came running?"

"It could have been work," I tell him.

"But, it wasn't," he says.

"But, it could have been," I tell him, adding, "You know those important things that you forget from time to time that I've always been here to help you with."

He laughs, says to me, "You act like you've taken care of me or something."

"Or something," I tell him.

He goes into the bathroom, cussing. Billy comes out a few minutes later, sits down at the dining room table next to me, and lights up one of my cigarettes. I fight the urge to not shut the computer lid. Drawing attention to something you want to hide is the first sure sign that you have something to hide. So, I pull up random websites and scroll through them, earning gift card points on a survey site as he sits next to me.

After several long moments of silence, he says, "So, I guess you know about tomorrow night then?"

That's when, and yes, John has impeccable timing, he responds. I nod at Billy, open the email and read, wearing the best poker face that I can find:

Honey, listen, my road hasn't been easy.

You've always been the bright light in all the dark.

And, now, you're even brighter.

There are so many things that I want to say and to do right now.

And, I know you just won't accept them.

Even the telling of them may make you run.

"So, what do you have to say about it?" Billy presses.

"I get that you say that you need this," I tell him. "But, if you want your family, this has to stop. She has to go away or I will go away, and you can threaten what you want. But, of all the people I never told about our life together, I will tell them all and have that courtroom filled with people on my side. Even if it takes making bargains with the devils in my family, I will do what I can to protect my boys."

"Right," he says, laughing. "So, you don't care that I need this."

I think a moment, gather up my thoughts, cross my hands on my computer, and tell him, with straight face, "I need my husband. And, if my husband isn't there, then, I have no husband."

"No," he's quick to correct me, "You have a husband that you've been neglecting, that you don't care about, and that you just want to see sitting here lonely and without sex."

I nod, reread John's message and hide it in the folder before speaking.

I tell Billy, "The moment we married, we have a contract, a contract. I've been faithful to that contract. You, on the other hand, have not."

And, the guilt teases the back of my thoughts.

"Like I said," he repeats, "You have a husband that you've been neglecting, that you don't care about, and that you just want to see sitting here lonely and without sex."

"So, what do you call what we did in the bedroom?" I ask.

"Painful," he says.

And, as hard as I try, I can't hide the fact that it's like he's slapped me repeatedly.

I say nothing. Billy jumps all over the silence.

"Right," he smiles, "I see you have nothing to say to that. Besides, you have to stop living in the past."

I nod, go back to a survey I had been doing, and ignore him.

Billy continues, because that's what he does, "So, I'm supposed to just sit here like I'm single and not be taken care of."

And, all that I had done in the bedroom was worthless.

I am worthless. To him, at least.

I swallow hard and tell him, "I do."

He blinks, shocked.

I dig in further with my insult, "Whenever I've gone without sex, when the boys needed me and I couldn't get away to get to you, I just assumed that you were going without it too. So, yeah, I've been living single for a long time, while you've been sucked and fucked by more than me. So, you want to fuck her, go ahead. I'm sure her tent has plenty of room for the two of you. Nice and cozy. And, wintertime's coming. You get a chance to keep each other warm."

He is speechless.

The direct approach not working, he tries the guilt and the manipulation.

Billy says, "Yeah, you don't love me. I never really thought you did and you just proved it after all."

I nod, seeing this approach, since I've been down this road repeatedly, and tell him, "If that's what you have to tell yourself in order to get by."

Which, I must add, is his own words that I've bundled up, repackaged and thrown back into his face. He swallows the insult, knowing exactly where it's come from, and sits smoking my cigarettes.

While I'm waiting for him to respond, I send John an email:

Tell me.

After I hit send, Billy responds, by saying, "You know you're almost out of cigarettes, what are you going to do when you're completely out? And seeing that I'm the one with money, I guess I would rethink that option if I were you."

"So," I tell him, "I'm supposed to allow you to fuck a prostitute that you're paying and my payment is cigarettes. Well, let me personally tally up your bill shall I? As I'm looking at it now, the few times, supposedly, that you've been laid by me is worth, what? Street value, at least to the junkies is $40, right?"

He thinks a minute, goes into his jean pocket and comes out with a hand full of change, in which he rummages through the change, finds a low denomination, and tosses it unto my computer. It's a nickel.

Billy tells me, "That's for tonight."

He then stands, takes several steps toward the living room, turns back, and tells me, "You want what you need, I suggest you allow me to do what I have to do and deal with it. Otherwise, you'll have nothing. You like throwing it up in my face that I'll have to live in a tent with her, try going without cigarettes."

"After all those years of me buying you cigarettes," I tell him, "This is the way that you treat me."

"You're not letting me get what I want," he says, adding, "So, let's take from you what you want."

"You already have," I tell him.

He laughs, says, as he's walking through the house, "That's a good flip. I've taught you well. That was good. I'm impressed. I'll be in my room, if you would like to negotiate this further."

He then goes to his room and my eyes go back to the computer screen.

John's reply waits for my attention.

I open the email and read.

I want to hold you, undress you, and give you the respect of a bed.

I want to take my time with you.

You're beautiful, baby. Listen to me, you're beautiful.

If you don't believe it, which I know you don't.

I want to make you feel beautiful again.

I hide the email, close the computer, and rest my head on top of the laptop. I take deep breaths and try to calm myself. Once you've convinced yourself that everything is fine, telling yourself that the chains you wear are necessary, and you get a glimpse of how thick the chains really are, it's a shock. And, it doesn't matter how many times you come face to face with the chains, the sight of them are always a shock. It's a mental game that you play. You're okay and then the sight of them sends you into a downward mental spiral. And, then, you convince yourself again and the shock happens yet again. Over and over and over again.

And people wonder why I have the anxiety attacks. They wonder where the PTSD came from, the illness, like it's mental and nothing more. I don't think it's mental. I think it's an emotional one. It's the equivalent of having someone take a hammer and beat your emotions repeatedly until it's so battered and bloodied that it becomes unrecognizable and you don't know how to feel anymore. It's emotional damage, not a mental illness.

That's where I am.

Sitting here, imprisoned to this life and to choices that I have no right to and no way of changing at the moment. Lied to and used, manipulated and yes, I will admit it to myself finally, abused, with the only option of sitting here in this forced witness status. No more. I can't take any more of it. My emotions are so beaten and bruised, so distorted and twisted that I can't utilize its gifts.

So, I come up with the only thing I can find that is optional and healing.

I open the computer and go to the hidden email. I take a shaky breath and write a response. I read the email through and reread to make sure it sounds right and hit send.

I need this and you.

If I can make a deal with the devil, will you be available tomorrow.

We can get a room. I'll pay my side, once I get the money.

But, I need this and you.

If you can stomach it for a moment.

I just need a moment. Please, if anything else, just one moment.

I wait for the response. When it comes, taking hazard looks across the room and down the hallway, to ensure I'm not being watched or that Billy isn't just coming out to be coming out, it's short and to the point. And, the tears catch in my throat.

My God, you have no idea who you are.

I write back, taking in the words and responding quickly.

I don't. Can you and will you help me?

I've never asked for help before, now I am.

I don't know what to say, it feels like I'm begging for sex.

I hit send and moments later, the response comes.

Don't beg. You have no reason to.

I'll see you tomorrow.

I have the room. No worries.

I'll take care of you.

I read the email and hurry another one and send, before shutting the laptop and planning out the next phase of my plan.

Thank you, honey.

I take a minute, collect my thoughts, and leave the dining room.

In the bedroom, he is lying in bed, cockily waiting for me to come in there. He hears me and doesn't look over.

Rather, he says, "I knew you'd come in here. It took you long enough."

"Right," I tell him, beginning, "I'm sorry. I'm sorry for the way that I acted. You're right, you need this. I only acted that way because watching this is hurting me." I swallow hard, choosing words that I don't mean out of the air, hoping, praying that he believes it, "I love you and I don't want to lose you. You have to take a minute and see it from my end and how I've been doing for you for years and then this happens. And, I'm now worthless and pushed to the side."

He exhales, throws a couple of cigarettes on the bed toward me, and says, "Here, smoke these and tomorrow come in and I'll give you money for cigarettes."

"Okay, thank you," I tell him, swallowing hard, and taking the cigarettes, adding, "I was wondering if I could ask something."

"Yeah," he says.

"Can I have my job back?" I ask, adding before he can argue my way out of it, "If I'm working then I'm not watching what you're doing and I won't argue with you about it and I'll be bringing money in and it will replace some of the money going out."

He thinks for a moment. I added the last part, sure he would take the bait, when he's so preoccupied with the money he has to spend on her and her sister, and on the countless others I'm sure, and as I watch, he focuses on the last. A huge smile crosses his face.

Billy tells me, "So, you'll be working so that I can pay to have sex with her?"

"Yeah," I tell him, through clenched teeth.

He laughs, says, "Awesome. That idea is enough to forgive you for the lies you just told in order to get cigarettes." He reaches over and flicks the ashes off, and turns back, saying, "But, that is an awesome idea. You should have told me that in the beginning and you would have kept your job. Fine, tomorrow, when you go to get cigarettes go up and talk to him about getting your job back."

"Thank you," I tell him.

"Right," he says, "Now get over and suck him. You don't have money as of yet."

An hour later, I'm going to bed and lying on the couch, thinking about how to do tomorrow. And, as I'm lying there, I can't sleep. Instead, I take a shower and reason with myself beneath the water's flow.

Chapter 14

Moment

I need one moment.

To be touched and felt, held and loved.

Just one moment.

           -but you are just as bad as he is

At least I'm not paying for it.

My God, how much money has gone out of this house?

           -but, you're making John spend money

           -on getting a room where you will fuck him

           -really, dishonest much?

           -and, the upside will be?

    -that you're rejected again and again and the memory will haunt

you

But, what if he doesn't reject you.

What if he wants to be with you?

What if it actually turns out okay?

What if the moment is a good one?

-how much hope have you wasted on other could be things?

-how many times have that hope been squashed?

But, this is different?

-how is it different?

-you're just as bad as he is

-doing this just to get laid

No, this is about more than that.

His is about getting laid.

Mine isn't.

I want to be touched and held, reminded that I'm alive.

Even if there is no sex, I need this.

I need him.

-what will you do with the guilt?

-how will you live with yourself?

-and what about the boys?

They need their mother.

And, in order for their mother to be here and able to care for them, I need to do this.

I need to undo what Billy has done.

Or, I will be raising my boys to be just like him.

And, if not just like him, to settle for stuff like this, like I have been doing.

I need to set my mind straight.

So that I can walk away.

-but, will you walk away?

-will you walk away?

-will you?

Chapter 15

The deceptive girl

The deceptive girl has reasons for being deceptive. She has a plan in mind and how selfless that she is, that plan is always centered on other people. Even when it appears that it isn't, that it's selfish and destructive, it does have others in mind. And, she has planned and planned and gone over the details in her mind. She has and is prepared for the worse to happen, as far as the worse that she can find in her imagination is concerned. For, life has its own way of destroying the security that that girl will find, wherever she manages to find it.

But, the deceptive girl has reasons and excuses, whichever you need at the moment that you need them. And, her reasons and excuses are understandable. You will agree with them and stand by them and even reassure her in her excusing and in her reasoning. And, yet, what you don't realize is that inside of her reasoning and her excusing is a little girl blaming herself and beating herself up for her decisions.

Even if there are plausible.

The next morning, my phone fully charged, I get the boys ready and off to school. Back at the house, I go into his room and he hands me money for cigarettes and tells me good luck. I wave and thank him and leave. I walk out of the house and shut the door behind me, taking every shaking step to outside of the Manor with my stomach in my throat and trying desperately to silence the guilt screaming in my thoughts.

I shouldn't feel guilty, I tell myself. I shouldn't feel guilty. Of all the things that he has done, I shouldn't feel guilty. But, I do, and I can't use his past behavior as the excuse for why I'm doing this. I just need to know that I'm human and alive again. Billy doesn't want me and because he doesn't, he's spent years making me not want me, teaching me how to hate myself and how to believe that every single little thing he has said were true.

Maybe, if he doesn't want me sexually, I'll bring out of this, at least, the ability to love me again, the ability to even look at myself again in the mirror without this profound hatred. And, of all the men I could have chosen, John won't hurt me. He will take care of me, of the few that I still trust and honestly I can't think of anyone else that I do, I trust John. I can be naked and vulnerable and honest in front of him and for him and with him.

I can be myself and not be rejected, not be hated for being me.

In order to keep some degree of truth, rather than email John right away, I head to Mike's restaurant and plan to just meet up with him there. Down the highway, I go over and over in my head what I will say and how I will approach him and what may happen. I'm nearly driven nuts by the time I reach the restaurant.

But, when I go in, I don't see John.

So, I speak to a few workers, put a bug in Mike's ear and he agrees to hire me back, and then I head outside to smoke. There, I send John an email from my phone.

I thought we had an appointment today.

You're not standing me up, are you?

Ten minutes later, Mike comes outside and approaches me, just as I light another cigarette. He's looking down, shaking his head, and nervously wringing his hands.

"What's the matter?" I ask him.

"We have to talk," Mike tells me.

"What's happened?" I ask.

"Let's talk," he says, pointing to a grass area under a tree across the parking lot. Close enough to walk to and far enough away from prying eyes and listening ears.

There, I ask him, again, "What's the matter?"

Mike looks down and back up at me, asking, "John didn't tell you anything about his life, did he?"

"A few things, here and there," I admit. This is when I embarrassingly think about my lack of inquiry into his life. He shared a few things with me, but, I didn't push the issue and I had been so self-absorbed that I hadn't noticed my oversight.

"Why?" I ask Mike.

"Well," he says, "I'll explain."

"Okay," I tell him, waiting for the other shoe to drop, if you will.

"He is coming," he tells me, "He just called me and said he's on his way and is taking you out of town."

I sigh and look away, half having expected to be told that he was going to ditch me or something. I couldn't have held it against him and I couldn't have gotten angry if he had. I really couldn't blame him at all if he does reject me.

Mike is nervous and looking at his feet again.

"What is it, Mike?" I ask, adding, "Whatever it is, you can tell me and you need to tell me if it has to do with John. Please."

"You know that when we were in school," he begins, "John went away to a music school."

"Yeah," I say, thinking of that afternoon I spent with him right before he left, and adding, to myself, "How could I forget?"

"Well," Mike says, "He went on to making music and having a career, a really good career. My little brother was famous, is famous," he corrects himself before continuing, "He's here because of you, but, he's here to recuperate, in a sense, and heal."

"What happened?" I ask.

"He made a few albums," he explains, "One of them he wrote about you, I'll give you a copy before you leave, and toured, and wrote music for others, sat in the background for many years, playing backup for other musicians, and then, he wrote this album and decided that he would tour smaller venues."

"Yeah," I say, wondering why I didn't know any of it. Wondering why he hadn't told me any of this. Wondering why I hadn't known about the album or the music or the career. And, why hadn't I asked?

"His opening night with the new album, a fight broke out in the club, a woman was caught in the middle of the fight and he jumped offstage to help her," Mike explains. "He was in the hospital for some time and we're still unsure if he's able to use his hand again, well enough to pick up a guitar. He has a career, an album to be proud of, an audience, a life he needs to get back to, and I personally don't want him here."

I look away, think for a moment and turn to Mike again, "Why are you telling me this?"

"I caught him the other night," he says, "He's staying with us and he was in the basement playing. His hand is fine. He just doesn't want to leave. At first I thought it was because of the memory of that night and being gun shy about being onstage, but, now, I'm not so sure."

I think for a long moment, piecing everything together in my head.

I tell Mike, "You think he's only here because of me."

"Yeah," he says, adding, "Sometimes, two people aren't meant to be together. They may fit and it may be perfect and they may be the best match for one another and will be able to give to one another exactly what they need when they need it and life will open up for the two of them. But, is it worth it if something happens to one of them down the road. That's why I think two people sometimes are just kept apart by fate and life and everything else. It may be good and great but it may turn out disastrous and be the worst thing for them both in the end."

"You want me to walk away and break his heart?" I ask.

"Give him today," Mike tells me, "And, then, walk away from him. Make him go back to all that he was and had before. He deserves better than this town, we all do, but, he actually got out and I don't want him coming back. He has a life out there, where we can't get out, he has. Let him go. If you love him, let him go."

Mike walks away from me and I stand there, replaying his words in my head.

I finish my cigarette and light another, knowing that he's right. I've been selfish and I've been blind and stupid and I'll give him today and if he leaves, it will be better for us both. Once Billy knows, and he'll find out what happens today, he will find out, if someone else doesn't tell him, I probably will. For, no matter what he has done to me, I still can't lie to him. But, once Billy finds out, John and I will be enemy. Especially John. And, the thought of what Billy can do scares me.

I sigh and let go of the need to hold onto John permanently. I'll take the moment and I'll hold onto for as long as I have breath.

A few moments later, John pulls up, smiles and gives his excuse. A waitress comes out with a bag that she presses in my hand. And, blindly and sadly, I get into the car with John and he pulls the car out into traffic, leading us off into the distance for the day.

In the car, he tries small talk and all I keep doing is thinking about having these upcoming moments and nothing more, just teasing my life and my heart for what I've not had and will never have again. The thought of just having him turn the car around and calling the whole thing off crosses my mind. But, I think that if I'm never to see him again, after today, at least we could give both of us today. Even if only today.

He pulls the car into a motel parking lot, somewhere in Delaware, just over the border and just out of Elkton, and gets out, opening the car door for me. I wait outside the office as he goes in and pays for a room and comes out, smiling, key in hand. I follow behind him, as he searches for our room, and I look around.

Take in the colors, the smells, and the vision of this place.

Take in the way he walks, how happy he is, and even the little things he says.

At the right door, he stops, inserts the key, and opens the door. I follow him inside and get a text message. It's Billy, of course.

Get the job back?

I text back, standing just inside the door, the only light that of my cellphone.

Yeah, not only did I get my job back, but I'm working for a few hours.

He replies, instantly, and a little too excited.

Awesome, I'll see you soon. Make lots of money.

I have plans for that money.

I fight the urge to not throw my phone and reply, quickly.

Right, see you soon.

I did not miss that, from Billy, there had been an absence of love, even in the emptiness of words, and only a hint of what he is to gain from me working. The guilt of the day is suddenly gone, becoming rather a longing and a sadness of loss, and John is still here. He's not gone yet and I'm longing for a moment we haven't had, as though I want to replay its every detail and slow down time to memorize even the insignificant details.

With the last message sent, I turn off my phone and cram it, along with the cd, into my backpack and set the bundle aside. The door is shut and locked behind me and John's hands are on my waist and my back and his lips on mine. There's whispers and touching and clothes tossed haphazardly throughout the room.

Sometime later, we're sitting on the bed, me in underwear and his t-shirt, and he's smiling, looking down at his hands. I try to memorize his face, hide there for a moment, and take in what I fear I will never have beyond this moment. My mind whispers that I should just take a picture on my cellphone of his face, but, I push it aside, fearful that the pain of that moment captured will make the picture worthless.

Better to engrave it into my mind than to keep physical evidence.

He looks up and over at me and keeps smiling.

He says, "I don't want to take you home."

That's when I find this door and step through it, leaving my heart behind in this room.

I tell him, "I have to go," looking down at the archaic blanket pattern, "maybe I shouldn't have done this."

"Feeling guilty," he says, choked up.

"A little bit," I tell him and I'm suddenly not lying.

"You have no reason to feel guilty," he tells me and still I do. But, I'm not guilty, surprisingly, of what I've done to my husband, because as far as I'm concerned he's not my husband anymore. Billy made his choice, and he choose himself and her; the rest is just paperwork. No, the guilt is centered on John and having to push him away, now that I don't want to let him go. Now that everything I need is right in front of me, I have to say goodbye and not look back.

He deserves more than this, more than me.

"I still do," I tell him, not looking at him.

John leans over and kisses my forehead, wraps his arms around me, like he doesn't want to let me go. I fight the tears and hold onto him for longer than I should have.

He breaks the embrace and tells me, "Come on, I'll take you home."

We leave the motel, getting in the car, in silence, and drive out of the parking lot. I turn, one last time, taking in the sight of the place where

I've left my heart and the exposure of trust that I didn't know that I had left for anyone, and attempt small talk. I hate small talk. It's a waste of words and time and isn't truthful no matter how hard you make it to be, small talk is just tiny lies all in the effort of talking, just to be talking.

"So, did you enjoy the day?" I ask. Yes, it's a stupid question. But, I couldn't come up with anything else to say. I hate small talk.

"I know what you're doing," John tells me.

"You do?" I ask, turning to face him.

"I do," he tells me, adding, "And, I don't like it. Please don't do that."

I swallow hard and ask, "What is it that I'm doing?"

"You're trying to fill in the space with conversation," he says. "I hate small talk, too. You don't have to do that, I'm telling you that you don't have to come up with something to say. And, if it's a question you sincerely do have, I've been looking forward to this day for a long time, and I don't want it to end."

I look down at my hands and swallow back the tears. I've come to the place where I can fight back the tears in front of Billy when he starts being a complete asshole, but, this is harder. I've never been in the place before and if I have, I just don't remember it anymore. When you have the light and the good and the dark floods in, and you are forced to live in the dark for so long, once the light appears, it takes some time for your eyes to adjust to the difference. And, I've been in the dark for so long, I was sure that any sign of the light would burn me to ash. Now, though,

I'm not ash, but, I want to cry and thank him for lying to me for the past few hours, apologize that he had to endure making love to someone like me, ask how he managed to do it without falling apart or running away, and hold onto him for dear life.

Instead, I look at my hands in silence, my fingers blurring slightly.

"You can cry," he whispers in the silent car. "You can. I won't stop you. I'll do what I can to make you happy again, but, there are happy tears, I know. And, I'll hope that they are happy tears."

I nod.

"Good," he says. John, then, reaches over and takes my hand. And, inside, I instantly turn to a ball of mush. The chains and the barbed wire, all of it collapse under this new pressure, this lightness of feeling, and I'm suddenly so uncomfortable that I want to scream in the silent car for him to turn around and go back.

I'm not ready to say goodbye yet.

Instead, I lean toward him a little, and stare at our hands intertwined.

Sometime later, we pass the border between Delaware and Maryland, entering Maryland and Elkton again, and my heart falls into my lap. It's almost over and this feeling will never happen again. John will be gone, as he should be, and I'll be a prisoner once again to Billy and his needs.

Rather than taking me home, as John wants to do, he drops me off at the Pizza place. We say little to nothing to one another when we part. Just a look, one long loving look of longing and I get out of the car, unable to say anything to Mike as I pass, walking down the highway, and toward home. Feeling the sensation of John attempting to follow me home, by the time I get to the light on Route 40 and Bridge Street, I close my eyes, pause in my steps, and beg God to have Mike influence John in doing the opposite. When I do hazard a look over my shoulder, my prayers had been answered. John had turned the car off, was getting out of the car, in a deep heated discussion with his brother. And, Mike had managed to convince him to come inside the pizza shop.

I sigh in relief and wait a few moments for the light, crossing Bridge Street, and heading down Route 40, toward home. Before I make it to the bridge, I can feel the ghost of his hands and his naked form on my body, taking his time and seeing me. I stop at the beginning of the bridge, hold on to its cement side, and collapse in tears.

The cars pass me by, each of their passengers accustomed to the sight, and ignoring my helplessness. For, I am just another woman crying on the side of Route 40. And, as far as their concerned, it is because of lack of drugs, my john not showing or showing, or life's hardships taking its toll. Either way, what the fuck do they care? I'm among thousands of just sights in this God Forsaken town.

I force myself to stand, take a few breaths, realize that the anxiety attacks haven't done this, and think. I focus on images in front of me: cars driving toward me and passed, faces blurred in each vehicle, the trees, and a few tents I see through the foliage.

That's when it hits me.

Her tent is out here, under the bridge somewhere.

The thought of going down into Tent City frightens the hell out of me. But, needing to know more about her, I swallow hard, and straighten my shoulders. I am ready to do what I have to do to find out, to seek some kind of closure in all of this. So, I look around, come up with a direct pathway in my head of how to make it down there and how to get back up again, and moments before I take a step, I see a figure emerge on the other side of the bridge, coming out.

It's her, tiny and petite and looking around, expecting someone. I hide in the bushes, and watch as she gets on her phone texting someone. She waits, texts again, and starts walking away, toward the Manor. I follow, at a distance, looking around, so as not to get caught by anyone. While following her, I come up with this strange plan. All I need is for both of them to follow through with their own stupidity in order for it to work.

She stops at the Liquor store on the corner of the entrance going into the Manor. I check my watch, I have two hours before the boys come home. Our vehicle has tinted windows, and the thought of getting caught gives Billy a rush, makes his dick harder than anything and with it being daylight, he's sure to take the chance. I hide by the bar and wait for him to pull up in front of the liquor store. There, they have this discussion, he parks around the corner, next to the bar and it takes quick steps for me to not get caught standing there, and both of them get out, walking toward the liquor store for something. That's when I take the opportunity and dive into the truck, hiding myself in the back, by floorboards, turning off my phone and hoping that Billy is a front seat guy.

Either way, I decide, if I'm caught in the Broncho, I'll beat the shit out of her and go down with a little respect, the way I want to anyway.

They come back some moments later, get in and he takes off, heading down the highway. He pulls into traffic, and they talk about her getting drugs and the fact that she's gotten two bags earlier, being a runner in order to earn them. Which, I calculate in my head, is about eighty dollars. She'll want more and he hands her money, like I knew he would.

They talk a little more and then get silent.

He makes one turn and then another. And, then, he whispers to her, with the turning signal glaring in the background and the vehicle and both of them waiting for what's coming next, "Let's see what we can get into here."

She laughs, a little teasing giggle, a little schoolgirl being flirted with and not knowing what the right reaction should be. I fight both anger and pain and find myself, instead, rolling my eyes and clenching my fists.

He makes the turn, onto a dirt road, I feel the truck bounce and the sound of the dirt on tires and her smoking his cigarettes. Then, he stops.

I venture a look.

He's pulled into a harbor of trees in the middle of nowhere.

How the fuck does he know about all the corners of my hometown when I don't?

Chapter 16

Pain and numb

The driver's seat is pulled all the way back.

The window raised.

The back of the seat reclined all the way.

Music playing in the background.

-I hate that fucking song.

He exposes his goods.

She giggles again, high and stupid and fucking idiotic.

There's kissing.

Her teeth are rotting out of her head and he's kissing her.

-but he complains about your breath in the morning

-right

A condom emerges, out of the wrapper.

She undresses, from the waist down.

Hits her head on the roof of the Broncho.

-karma hurts huh bitch?

-just get high again, the pain will go away

-and it won't matter who you were fucking

She crawls across, positioning herself on the center console.

Her knees on the console, with her naked ass in the air.

On the console where our kids play.

On the console where we've set food for them.

On the console where he's held my hand, in those rare moments.

-yeah, but it's not about me, right?

-I've just made this all about me

-this has nothing to do with hurting me and our boys

-oh no, it's all about you

-you narcissistic fucker

The condom is on, she's sucking.

He's playing with her ass and he's rubbing her sweet spot.

I hear her moan.

He gasps, breathing heavy, gasps more and more.

-there are no complaints

-he doesn't object to her method

-getting off on her tiny mouth on his sex

-while I've sucked for hours, changing it up, obeying to the smallest detail

-and all he's done has complained

-for hours, complaining

-I was sure I was just doing it wrong

-for years, I thought I was unable to give pleasure

-to be pleasurable to anyone

-until this afternoon

-until now

For the length of a song, she sucks and he gasps.

His eyes closed.

Playing with her sweetness, looking at and admiring her ass.

For the length of a fucking song.

Then, he taps her ass, giving her the go ahead to get on top.

I watch her move into position, getting loud with his insertion.

He lifts her hips and guides her up and down, loud sounds of pleasure on both sides.

-in the seat where our boys have sat

-playing with the steering wheel

-playing with the radio

-in the same fucking seat where they've been

-where he's promised to teach them to drive

-told them he loves them

Now he gives her sweet nothings.

-and it becomes too much

-if you don't want me

-fucking tell me you don't

-if you don't get off with me anymore

-fucking tell me you don't

-don't destroy me in the process and have me need to confirm your lies

-don't have me need to have sex with someone else

-just to find out that I am worth more

Soon there is wet slippery rocking, with the playing of a new song.

And, I formulate a crazy, mixed up plan.

And, I don't really plan.

Its anger, with the sounds of her pleasure and his and the sight of her grasping.

Grasping and riding and the stopping and kissing between them.

And, the fact that it's in the seat, in the truck where our boys have been and grown.

Where they've loved daddy and looked up to him.

In the seat where they've played.

In the truck where they've been protected.

That's why.

And, suddenly, there is nothing more.

She bites her lip, just as I jump over the seat, and fucking punch her square in the face.

Chapter 17

The angry girl

When your woman is angry enough to beat another woman's ass, either she's worth keeping or you need to be petrified, to say the least. Now, when that same woman has been under your thumb for years, listening to you lie to her of how inadequate she is in bed and out and then suddenly she's able to face you and the other woman with fists clenched, fearing no one, there is another man in her life. And, if you don't realize this, you're stupid and don't deserve her anyway. For, she's learned to stand strong from somewhere. She's learned that you've been lying to her, from somewhere. Someone else has made love to her and told her that she isn't inadequate in bed. Someone else has made love to her and reached multiple climaxes, coming back for more.

That new angry girl will kill her liar, if need be. Remember that.

Billy doesn't have time to react. I am on her and beating the hell out of her, while he's still in the midst of guiding her hips. I drag her ass off of him and leave the condom behind. Oddly enough, I think that if her pussy was so tight, you would think that she'd take the condom with her. No, and I laugh at the sight, that and the shocked expression on his stupid face.

I manage to open the passenger side door and drag her out by the head of her hair, get her down on the ground, where I proceed to beat her about the face and body. In the corner of my eye, he's adjusting himself and getting covered and getting out, taking his time to walk around the truck. I stop when he comes close enough to do something. And, rather than letting her squirm and run to his aid, I take her clothes from the truck and throw them at her.

I tell her, "Get dressed, you fucking whore."

He stands there, a minute, watching.

She stands, goes to swing at me, and I stand, not flinching, staring her down.

"I dare you," I tell her.

Instead, she gets dressed, whining to him, saying, "You going to let her do this shit? I mean, you paid me and she acts like it's my fault. You going to let her hurt me like this? Don't you care about me?"

I laugh, in the uncomfortable forming of this trio, I laugh.

"She's fucking crazy," she whines to Billy, "Why is she laughing?"

I look at Billy and tell her, eyes on him, "Because he doesn't about you at all, bitch. The only person he cares about is himself, what he can get and when he can fucking get it. You seriously think he doesn't have a backup plan to you, you're sadly mistaken."

Billy smiles and says nothing.

"You fucking bitch," she screams, "That's not true, he just told me."

I turn to her and ask her, "Told you what? That he loves you? That he cares about you? That he'll take care of you? That you make him so hard? That he wants you like he's never wanted anyone before? Really? Do you think you're the first one he's said that, too? Did you think he would kick me out and let you fucking move in, away from your tent, with built in money bags to get you drugs whenever you want them? Guess what? I pay the fucking rent, bitch. That house, is mine, and my kids. Not his. And, this truck, I fucking bought that too. The truck you're fucking in, it's mine. And, his dick that you think you have control over. He doesn't want to divorce me and thinks in his little mind that I'm going to roll over and let him do as he pleases. But, he is scared of what I will do to him. Child support alone will break him and he has nowhere to go. Where's he going to go? Your tent?"

I laugh again. And, look at Billy. His face is pale. I am right.

Suddenly the inner shaking is gone.

I'm not afraid anymore.

She stands there, having had listened to me and turns to him for reassurance.

She asks him, "Tell me she's lying. The truck is yours right?"

He looks down.

I can't help the grin on my face.

"The house is yours," she goes on. "Tell her you're kicking her out. Tell her, you want me to be there and not them."

He looks down.

I can't help myself. I say, "Go ahead, tell her. Tell her that you're willing to never see your kids again and pay rent on your own to feed her money for drugs and to slowly lose everything just for that pussy."

He looks away, uncomfortable, wiping his face, unable to look either of us in the eye.

"Tell her," she demands. "Tell her what you told me, that you don't want her, you want me. Tell her, babe, tell her."

"Yeah, babe, tell her," I press.

Still, he says nothing.

I look at her, smiling, and reach back and punch her in the face, knocking her ass out. As she lays unconscious on the ground, I look down, feeling nothing.

I tell her still body, "That's for being so fucking stupid."

I look at him, shake my head, and say, "Go ahead and try to get me locked up on the fourth floor. I'll chew you up and spit you out. Try me."

He smiles at me, says, "I'm not going to do that."

"Right," I tell him, adding, "Like I believe any fucking thing you have to say at this point."

I take out my phone and tell him, "One call to the cops is all I have to do. She goes to jail and so do you."

"For what?" He asks. "Drugs?" He looks down at her and adds, "She has it on her, but, what are you going to tell them about the state of her face? She's pretty fucked up, isn't she? Make you feel good, didn't it? To know that you won this fight? So fucking what?"

She comes to at this moment, sitting up slowly and complaining of her head hurting.

"You're right," he continues, "I couldn't care less about her, about either of you. Like there's not more of her on the streets that I can find at any given moment."

"And, you have the numbers to prove it," I finish Billy's thought.

"There you go," he says, looking down at her, "Now she gets it and me."

She slowly sits up and says, "Are you fucking kidding me?"

I laugh and turn to walk away, saying over my shoulder, "You are fucking stupid, you know that?"

"Who the hell you calling stupid?" She demands, adding, "You married him."

"Yeah," I reply, "We all make mistakes, don't we?"

I walk away, down the little dirty lane, and shortly after, while sometime later, he did have to get his money's worth, after all, they pass me in the truck. I know that's what he's done because I'm nearly to Route 40, on foot, by the time they pass me, both of them in the truck and she's smiling. He's given her extra money for her trouble and she's fucked him anyway, even after all of that. I wonder, as I see them drive pass, how many lies he's had to give to her in order to get the completion of his order?

I push it all away and suddenly feel defeated.

For, it doesn't matter what I've done, he still managed to do what he wanted to do anyway. By the time I get home, I'm in time to get the boys off the bus. While walking them home, I text Mike:

Did he go?

His one word reply settles everything for me, instantly.

Yes.

I'm nearly at the front door, when Mike sends another text message. This one I'm not expecting, even as I'm thankful that John is gone, and sad for that same reason. The message, though, reflects everything in its miniscule size.

Thank you.

I fight the tears away and find it hard, now, to be as brave as I was an hour before. There are too many factors now at play. And, home, alone, with Billy, the tides could turn again. I know that, above and beyond, all else, I'm going to pay for my earlier outburst. How, though, I'm not sure.

And, this worries me.

But, going into the house, Billy is all smiles and as nice as he can possibly be, and as nice as he has been in quite some time. He plays with the boys, takes time to ask about their day, and even has their favorite snack waiting for them. I look around, confused. He smiles at me and in the midst of laughing and joking with the boys, says something to me that is meant to settle it all but merely puts me on edge.

He says, "I learned my lesson today. I married the one that I want and that settles that."

But, still he doesn't look at me when he says this. And, I'm split between believing him and being on guard, waiting for the other shoe to drop.

That night is blissful, if there is any such thing, in all of the chaos that is our marriage now. I'm on guard and find myself, literally, sleeping with one eye open, even as I sleep on the couch. The boys are asleep in their rooms, after a family meal and laughing and ice cream afterwards. Then, late in the night, as I am sleeping, but, not sleeping, I hear his phone go off.

A text message. From her.

And, then, moments later, it goes off again.

I creep down the hall and stand at the door. From where our bed is located in the room, he doesn't know that I'm standing at the door, and I see him texting her. Back and forth the texts continue. Then, he says to himself that he guesses he's going out. And, that the day he's just given to me, I should be thankful for that. Going to her, is the least that he can do, after all that I had done earlier that day. He sits up, on the edge of the bed, and I creep back to the couch and lay back down.

Moments later, I hear him coming down the hallway, and stopping in the living room, just in front of the couch. For long moments, he stands there, unmoving. I keep my eyes closed, fearful of what is about to happen. Then, he speaks.

"I know you're awake," Billy says. "And, I know you heard it go off. You heard my phone."

I open my eyes and look at him.

"It's the least that I can do," he tells me, to my face, which by this point I'm not surprised by anything, "After all that you did to her, earlier today."

I smile, still proud of myself, and ask, "Is she sucking dick the way she used to?"

"Better," he says, shrugging his shoulders, "You actually did me a favor. Now, I don't have to pay as much as I did before. Now, she comes to me, fearful that she's going to lose me. Grant it, I still pay her, you pay for service, especially when they're worth it."

With that, he leaves, and the entire day vanishes in one puff of exhaled cigarette smoke.

I wait until the Broncho is completely gone before I make it to the dining room and to my computer. There, I check my email.

There is, among all the other nonsense, one email that I've been hoping for.

It's from John.

Today, I've been waiting for this moment for a long time.

Thank you for trusting me enough to know that I wouldn't hurt you.

I'm playing a club tonight.

I'm back in New York, not because I left you, but because you've given me the ability to try again, to be more and to do as I know that I should be doing.

Please, know that I'm still here, and you're all that I want.

All that I've ever wanted.

I need to do this, Mike is right. Please, tell me, you're okay.

I read the email several times and smile to myself. Because of me he was able to face his fears and get back onstage. That's all I wanted. I've given him that much. I pushed him away and he's worried about losing me. But, he's onstage again. He's onstage and trying and succeeding, I know.

I look at the time: its 2 a.m. his set must be long over. But, he's probably busy, with some tag along, some other woman that will be to him more than I could ever be. I shake my head and send the email anyway, hoping to not hear anything back, hoping that she is preoccupying him the way I had earlier that day.

You need to be there.

I need to be here.

When we are meant to be in the same place, we will be.

I go to close my computer, sure that Billy will be gone some time, and not wanting to sit there like a little school girl waiting for a response I'm hoping both that does come and doesn't come. But, just as I go to close the computer, I get an email back.

You pushed me away.

You weren't feeling guilty, were you?

You wanted me to do this, to come here, to chase after my dreams again.

You wanted me to come here?

I don't understand.

I touch the screen and say aloud, "Because that's what you do when you love someone. And, I do, I love you, honey."

I sit back and think about what I've just said and realize that it's the first time that I've been able to feel that way, comfortably, knowing that I wouldn't get hurt, physically, mentally, emotionally, in return. I am allowed to love. I have been given this chance to love and finally be loved in return. Even at a distance, I'll take it. Even if it is mere crumbs that I've been given. Hell, I've survived and managed to push through on far less than those diamonds of crumbs.

I think hard about what to reply and finally settle on:

That's what you do.

He replies back, instantly.

When you love someone?

Say it, please. Just say it, after today and tonight, say it.

That's all I need to push through and do this without you physically here.

Just tell me how you feel.

Say it, sweetie, say it.

I read and reread the message and want to say it so badly. But, that would bring him back, at least mentally and his mind needs to be 100 % on what he's doing at all times. So, I refrain. Rather, I send this message:

Tell me how it went tonight.

There is some time before I get a response. When it comes, I'm in tears.

It was beautiful, like coming home.

It was the second best thing I've known.

It was like holding you over and over again, safely.

With no one interrupting us, just the two of us.

That's how it felt tonight.

You've given me that. Thank you, sweetie.

"Good," I say aloud, repeating this one word over and over again. Then, to redirect his attention, or so I tell myself. It's only after I send the next message that I realize that my intentions are completely different, that I'm actually gaging how he really feels about me.

> *Aren't you supposed to be entertaining some groupie or something?*

This reply is instant.

> *I'm too damn old for that shit, Ronnie.*

> *Seriously, been waiting a long time for you.*

> *Why the hell would I screw it up with some nameless groupie?*

> *I've been there, done that, and know the difference.*

> *But, thanks for the under table test there, clever that one was.*

> *It's okay, after everything he's done to you, test me as much as you like.*

> *I've waited this long, I'll go through the tests and prove myself.*

> *I swear.*

I shake my head and find that I'm enjoying someone that knows me that well. I send another message, smiling through tears.

> *I know, I had to, I can't explain.*

> *Maybe I just shouldn't try.*

> *Anyway, think of me, dream of me, I will be doing the same of you.*

He responds, immediately.

Get some rest. I will be doing the same.

I love you, more than you know.

Against my better judgment, I reply.

Me too.

And, close the computer.

I go back to the couch and try to sleep, but, can't. I'm fearful of what will happen when he returns and end up pacing the floor all night. Thankfully, he doesn't return, that night or the next day until right before the boys are home from school. Two hours before I am to be at the bus stop to pick them up, he walks in, says nothing, and goes straight to the bedroom, gathers clothes and goes to the bathroom. I hear the shower turn on and watch the clock, wondering if I should just leave. Take a walk, wait for the boys and not come back without them.

Then, I wonder if I should even bring them back. My mind searches desperately for an alternative and come up with two neighbors that I can send them to. Just in case. There, with either neighbor, they won't be suspicious, they won't ask questions, and will have other children to play with. But, which one? I decide on one and have my decision, I at least have that taken care of, in my mind.

When he does get out of the shower and dressed, I'm standing in the kitchen, cleaning up. I'm refusing to look him in the eye and keep doing what I'm doing, pretending to be oblivious of him standing there, watching me, with this amused expression on his face.

"Well," Billy says, "I haven't seen this before."

"What is that?" I murmur, expecting the insult to come. And, sure enough, it does.

"You cleaning," he says and laughs at his own joke.

"Funny," I tell him.

"I thought so," he says, adding, "Just as funny as telling the cops about your little discretion yesterday and the restraining order they granted her for you to stay away from her. Oh, and that includes me, so I guess you won't be staying here, huh? And, if you're wondering about the kids, they stay, you don't."

I drop the rag in my hand and tell him, "You're lying."

"I'm not," he says, handing me a few sheets of paper.

I start reading them, the restraining order, the court document, the giving of custody to him, the deal that rather than pay child support, I'll have to just keep paying rent and not being able to live here. Here, the house that I'm paying for, where my boys are, the boys I gave birth to, that I raised. That I have to walk away or go to jail. I have no other choice.

I look up at him and ask, "What the hell did you do?"

He smiles, tells me, "I made my choice, remember?"

"But, you're wanting her here, a junkie, to raise our boys?" I ask.

"My boys," he says. "You don't want to play by the rules, well, I'll force you to one way or another."

"They're my boys," I tell him. "You can't take them from me."

"I'm not," he says, "You are. You've done this, I didn't."

I am confused and can't look away from the paperwork. Court documents forcing me out of my own home, of the home I share with my boys. Their home. Their life. The life I've fought to give to them. No, I tell myself. Of all the things you have done, you will not do this to me or to them.

"Right," I tell him, "What do you want me to do?"

"Stay out of the way," he tells me, adding, "And, all of this will disappear."

And, in order to keep my boys and my house and my right to raise them, protecting them from the junkie and the insanity that their father has become, I make a deal with the devil. I know, instantly, that I will not be able to fully keep my side of the deal as every deal with the devil changes to benefit the devil. I know, too, even as the words leave my mouth, that I am alone in protecting my boys.

I am alone.

"I will do whatever you want me to," I tell him, numbly.

My voice sounds strange and far away and as soon as I say the words, there is this unusual shiver that goes down my spine. I suppress the shiver and look to Billy who smiles and nods and takes the paperwork from my hands.

"It doesn't matter who she is," he tells me, "It's just about you understanding that this is what I want. You've made me suffer long enough and I just need this."

"How did I make you suffer?" I ask.

"We were good," he tells me, "In the beginning and then the kids came and it was all about them. I don't have time, I have to take care of them."

I stop him, putting my hand up as to silence his excuse.

"I can understand that," I tell him, adding, "If you weren't their father and you came along just recently. But, that excuse doesn't fly with me anymore. It doesn't. You are their father and you've been here from the beginning, and you wanted them as much as I did and do. So, next excuse, that isn't selfish and narrow minded."

He face flushes red and I wonder what my punishment will be for that truthful hurt.

"That's the excuse I'm going with," he smiles, adding, "I could tell you how terrible you are in bed or how you've let yourself go and gained weight."

"I'm smaller now than when we first met," I correct him, adding, "Maybe it's just because you're addicted to whore the way she is addicted to heroin."

For this, I feel the sting and jerk of his hand meeting the back of my head. My ears ring and I choke back the tears. I clench my teeth and leave the house, going after the boys. Just as I open the door to leave, I stop and turn, saying one last thing to him.

"You're the only one that's gained weight, fat boy," I tell him, adding, "And, it's sad that you have to pay for sex outside of our relationship, since I'm so disgusting. You know you have to pay for it, me on the other hand, well, I've gotten laid and no money exchanged hands, at least, not from mine."

I walk out the door, as he slams a glass against the wall. At the bus stop, I wait for their bus to arrive, shaking from head to toe. The pain is a knot in my chest and in my stomach. I can't think straight and fight the desire to go back to the house, in some odd attempt to go back in time, to when I thought we were happy, to this faded image of what we were in times past. And, I have to tell myself, standing there, faking a smile to my friends, my only friends, during the only times I can socialize with anyone, that the past ten years was one huge lie. That he never wanted me, never loved me, and I've been living this lie, believing that everything was perfect and fine and good.

Sometime later, just as their bus is pulling up and stopping, Billy drives out of the street, squealing wheels to make it obvious how angry he is. I sigh in relief that he's gone, for at least a little while. Maybe, by the time he goes out and hunts her down and fucks her, he'll come back calmer and the boys may be asleep by then. By the time he comes in and has a less loud and angry fight than what would have been had he have stayed and waited for me to return, without going out and finding her and doing what they do.

Maybe, I think oddly, she's an asset after all.

The boys and I have a quiet evening, as I come up with yet another excuse to cover up the fact that their father is gone for the night. By the time Billy returns, the boys are asleep and their clothes are laid out for the next morning for school.

Billy comes in, slamming the door, and giving me an angry, moping glare that is meant to have me apologizing. Instead, I blow him off and ignore him. He stomps through the house, goes to his room, once our room, and minutes later returns, slamming through the kitchen and attempting at getting my attention. When he realizes nothing is working, he sits down at the dining room table next to me, smoking.

"So," he says.

"So," I say.

"She was good tonight," he says.

"I'm glad," I tell him, unmoved.

"She was nice and tight and wet and willing to do anything," he continues.

"I'm glad for you," I tell him, as believable as I can be.

"And, I did things tonight with her I've never done with another woman," he tells me.

"What was that?" I ask, sarcastically, adding, "Did you hold her hand and whisper sweet nothings to her?" And, before he can respond, I continue, "Oh, no, wait, I know what you did, you held her all night and watched her favorite movies, right. Oh, no, wait, I know what you did, you gave her oral rather than whining and complaining and demanding and threatening until you received oral repeatedly, until you felt that you were satisfied. Oh, no, wait, I know what you did, you told her you loved her and meant it."

While he smiles and leans back in his chair, pretending to laugh, I continue.

"Is that what you did?" I ask. "Or, no wait, I know, you took her out to dinner and treated her like a lady. Now, that's what I believe that you've never done with a woman. So, which one was it and how did it go, sweetheart?"

With that, Billy stands from the table and pushes his chair in.

He says, "I knew I married a bitch, I just didn't realize how much of one you really are."

"Right," I tell him, because at times I don't know how to just let him have the last word and walk away, "And being chained to you, after everything you have done, is so my idea."

Billy turns back and glares at me, saying, "Aw, is mommy upset with her living conditions? Maybe jail would be all the better for her complaining ass?"

"And that's supposed to upset me?" I ask. "Like jail is far worse than living with you. You have to ask yourself why you would continually want to be chained to a woman that is such a horrible experience for you. You know, why don't you just jump in and run away with your homeless junkie? What? Tent life not appealing to you?"

"Is it to you?" He asks, smiling.

I decide to do something I've never done before. I bluff.

"I pay rent here," I tell him, adding, "Therefore, the house is mine. And, you're not willing to pay rent and if you think that I can't fight and win those ridiculous court papers, if they even exist at all, and win, you're mistaken. And, if you think that I don't have an attorney already, you are also mistaken."

The first part is true, the last about the attorney was all a bluff. I hadn't realized that I could actually take that step until the words left my mouth, in an attempt to simply win the argument. It is only then that I tell myself to take note and to get a fucking attorney as soon as I possibly can.

Deals with devils are exercises in futility.

Billy, rather than taking the bluff and simply walking away, sits down on the arm of the loveseat, located at the entrance into the living room, and folds his arms. He takes a moment, weighing his options and begins his usual, backdoor approach in making me feel bad, or attempting to do so. At this moment, I'm glad the boys are asleep and not able to hear us.

"If only you would have still been the wife you were in the beginning," he says, sadly.

"What? The one without children?" I ask him, straight face, still angry that he would dare use our boys as an excuse to hurt me repeatedly, to do what he was doing and refuses to stop doing.

"No," he says, adding, "The obedient wife that never questioned anything."

I laugh, not realizing that I actually have a laugh in me to project and the sound is strange and alien. I tell him, "Right, and, you haven't had anything to do with that. Let me put it to you this way, sweetheart, if a woman starts out a relationship with you, sweet and innocent and ends up a bitch at the end and this occurs with ten, twenty, thirty women, by that time, maybe you need to sit back and ask yourself what the common dominator is. Is it just that they're women and will end up bitches no matter what?"

With this, he smiles and nods, proudly.

"Or," I continue, having expected him to respond this way, "is it that they've become bitches because of you, since of all the unrelated women you've been with, you are the only common link to them all. Therefore, you've turned them into bitches and it's the damage that you've caused that has brought them to the point of who they are."

Billy laughs, says, "Of course it is and they were so good to me, all of them were."

I nod, tell him, "After all this time of us being together and knowing how I've changed, I now believe that, that all of us were good to you, as good as each of us could have been. The ones that stayed longer with either dumber, which is the one I'm leaning towards, or have more patience than the others. And, if this last were true, I'm more fucking patient than I thought."

"You were the patient one?" He asks, laughing. "You were the one needing patience, right. Oh, that's nice, that's clever, like you didn't open the door and push me out, and making me go find something quick and easy and ready to go at any minute?"

"Something that you have to pay for and track down?" I ask, adding, "How is that actually that fucking easy?"

"I'd rather track her down," he has the nerve to tell me, "And even pay her, than to hear her complain and throw a fit that I want time with her. No, with the right amount she's good to go."

"Because the only responsibility that she has," I inform him, "is finding her fucking heroin."

"Yeah," he says, adding, "I'm good with that."
I laugh and shake my head.

"Why are you laughing?" Billy has the nerve to ask me.

"Why do you think?" I ask.

"I have no idea," he says, telling me, "You're the one with your balls nailed to the wall, I see nothing funny in the way things are going."

"I find it funny," I inform him, "That you think I'm the one with my balls nailed to the wall."

And, just as he is trying to explain how much control he suddenly has, I stop him, and say, "Whatever way you think this is going, you're wrong. I'm laughing, because I am really sure you don't get this. You don't. See, you have loaded your wife down with responsibility, many of those responsibilities, most husbands manage to do themselves, and yet you cannot do them alone. And, after you've loaded her down, you complain that she doesn't have time for you. So, you make it impossible for her to give you time, add more shit to her plate and use that as the excuse to fuck around with a homeless, junkie prostitute. Right. Logically speaking, asshole, you wanted it this way and there, you got it, I don't have all this time for you because I'm taking your burden off your shoulders to give you rest and the ability to take a minute after working. While, you are off fucking with that thing. So, you wanted it from the beginning, go with it, then, and stop complaining about it, stop using it as a tool to make me feel guilty because things turned out the way you've made them. You wanted this from the beginning, congratulations you got what you want. Yet again."

"Yeah, I did," he admits, then adds, "I wanted a good lay and that's what I've got now."

"Right," I tell him, "And, she has to be high in order to fuck you. My lay was free and he didn't have to be high and didn't want me to leave and I don't have to track him down."

I had to say it, it was there and it was open and I had to do it. Digging it in was worth it, believe me, it was so worth it. To see his face turn pale and then go red in rage and to glare, his eyes narrowing and his arms unfolding. Definitely worth it. Whatever happens afterwards, that was worth the risk.

"What the fuck did you just say to me?" He demands.

"Oh, you didn't get that?" I ask, smiling. "My lay," I repeat, "didn't have to be high in order to fuck me, nor did I have to track him down. He didn't want me to leave and, oh, the best part about it is I didn't have to pay him to fuck me. It was free because he wanted to fuck me and did, repeatedly, without complaint. I had all the time in the world for him because when we were getting together to fuck, he didn't have a long list of things for me to do ahead of time. You know, like you have to call my doctor before we do anything. You have to clean the house first, do more laundry, because that's the only way you turn me on."

"That does turn me on," he tells me, angrier.

"Then, what turns you on when it comes to her?" I ask, adding, "Because we both know she doesn't know what a fucking broom is or a washing machine. She gets all her clothes for free from social services, when she's up there whining the poor mouth that she's homeless. It's funny that they don't take the time and ask her why she's homeless. That they don't care to even realize that she's chosen this lifestyle for herself, the way you have."

He glares at me, unable to speak. For the first time in ten years, he is speechless.

"Right," I decide to dig it in even deeper. Billy does deserve it, after all. "Like I was saying, he was free, and willing and very able and did things that you'd never do to even the one you're fucking paying and hunting all over the place for. And, he has money and wants to take care of me and the boys and I think I'll let him."

Quietly, Billy says, "A marriage can't survive without sex, honey."

"First off," I tell him, "I'm no longer your honey, your babe, your sweetheart, I'm nothing more to you than a prisoner. That's all I am. I'm the cause of all your problems, remember? Not the homeless junkie prostitute that's fleecing you for her drugs so that you get your rock soft. Not her, me, I'm the cause of all your problems. And, second, you should have thought about that before you started pushing me away, when I would go in and love on you and make passes at you and you'd push me away, tell me you were tired and that I needed to do this and that. You should have thought about that, then. You have no one to blame but yourself for this. You made this decision. You placed the cards on the table the way they're sitting, and yet you blame me for the way they've been dealt when I haven't laid hands on the deck."

"That's nice," he says, quietly, "That you would blame me for all of this."

"It is you, all you," I tell him. "Take responsibility for your actions and admit what you've done. Teach your boys, at least, what it means to be a man that's fucked up and willing to admit that he's fucked up. Rather than teaching them to chase after a fucking homeless junkie whore who has had so many men that she doesn't even know how many and all just to fucking get high."

I sit there for a moment, quietly thinking, watching him act like he is about to cry. And, I suddenly realize that I've faced him without anxiety attack. That's what has been missing all day, the lack of anxiety, and the peace behind the decision. I know what and who I want and I'm not doing this anymore. I may have made a deal with the devil for my boys, but, my heart belongs to another man, a good man that I've sacrificed any selfish need I have to be with him, hide myself in his existence, so that he can go fulfill his dreams. That's when I'm able to say, with the most peacefulness I've ever had when it has come to facing Billy, the truth of what I now believe.

"But, that's okay," I tell him, "What you won't teach them that they truly need to be good men, another man is able to and will, because I know him and he is a good man, where you're not. So, at least, I can say that my boys will be taught to be good men, just not by their father."

I wait for a reaction. And, his facial expressions reveal nothing.

I'm so at peace with what I've just told him, that I don't see it coming.

Billy reacts so quickly, moves so fast, that I don't even have enough time to brace myself for the impact.

Chapter 18

Physical pain and losing hope

When your back hits the wall, swallow the pain.

When his fists punch the brick above you, don't flinch.

When he picks you up and throws you down the hall, don't scream out.

The boys are sleeping

Let them sleep

When he picks you up and pins you against the wall, don't look away.

When he has his hands around your throat, don't struggle for air.

You've been good

You've given birth to good boys

They will love the right way

They will carry on

Where you do not

When he punches holes in the bedroom door, don't be intimidated.

Don't pray for protection, not anymore.

Just pray that they don't wake

Let them sleep, God, please, don't wake them

When he throws you into the bedroom, don't fight to get out.

When he forces you onto the bed, don't fight his angry hands.

Don't listen to his lying words.

Let peace reign

Please, I need peace

Don't take that from me, now

When he strips the clothes off of you, scratching you and bruising you, don't cry out.

When he pulls your hair and buries your face in the bed, don't fight to breathe.

When he forces himself inside of you, don't move.

Don't be happy that at least it is though he wants you.

He doesn't want you.

It is the same as it was back then.

This is rape.

Just don't remember that time before.

Don't slip into the attack

Don't allow the quirk to come and take over

Don't panic

Just think about John and his hands and him taking his time

Hide there

Don't think about this

Don't realize what is happening

Not yet

Not yet

Not yet

When he's done, don't cower in a corner.

Keep the stone face, remember gentle hands taking his time on your body.

Remember the peace, the moments stolen.

Just take your clothes and leave the room, quietly.

Let him win for the moment.

Take the walk of shame out of the room as he tells you you're nothing.

Don't believe him.

You are something important to someone

Your boys need you to be strong

Be strong for another moment

Take the walk of shame out of the room.

Down the hall.

To the bathroom, clothes in hand, and shut and lock the door behind you.

Turn the shower on and only then, beneath the rush, only then can you fall apart.

Fall apart

Help me do this

Please don't leave me now

Please God I need You

Don't leave me

Don't remember that of long ago.

This is different.

This is different, isn't it?

And, when he unlocks the bathroom door, opens the curtain, don't cry.

Gather the pieces together quickly and harden yourself.

When he gloats over what he's done, don't flinch.

No tears, he hates that.

Let him watch you, don't cry.

Let him brag about it all and complain about how awful a lay you were.

Just don't cry.

Don't fall apart.

Your boys need you

Your boys need you

Remember that

You need John

Hide in that stolen moment

That is love and sex, not this, not this

That was peacefulness

You deserve the peace

Just don't cry, he hates that.

Chapter 19

The hooking girl

When all else fails, become what you hate.

That's pretty much all I have to say about that. I can't explain the smallest steps leading to this. But, Billy embraced his junkie and took in the junk himself. He lost his job, shortly after, and began stealing from the house and the boys' piggy banks to get high and to pay her for another go around. Having been abandoned by everyone, there was no one there to help me and no office would help and no law enforcement would even arrest him, let alone drug test him, and I was so focused on keeping myself calm that I never got the attorney. All I had on my mind was keeping the boys in the dark about it all. Keeping them happy and content, taking care of them the best way that I could.

But, I had to do something and working was not an option.

When I attempted to go back to work at Mike's pizza shop, Billy showed up demanding that I steal from Mike to aid both his habits. When I refused, he choked me in the parking lot. Even then, the cops did nothing. They just shook their head at me and one of the cops I had gone to church with years before. At the time, I shook my head at their superior shaking heads and told the former church associate police officer a little tidbit that he did not approve of.

"It must be refreshing to know that you are that kind of Christian," I told him.

Both cops left, laughing, telling each other that I deserved the choking. When they were gone, Marie and Mike both fired me, adding that John was doing well and I had made the right decision in letting him go. They added that they were sorry, but, it had been the best for everyone involved.

From then on, I gave up on working.

Instead, I do this, standing in a motel room, working out the details with yet another former schoolmate.

"How long do I have?" He asks, taking off his shoes.

"An hour," I tell him, hoping he won't take that long.

"Right," he says, smiling, socks off next, and then shirt.

"So, what first then," I remove shirt and bra and pants and underwear, and pile them on top of my shoes in the corner. "The bed?" I ask.

He nods, stands and unbuttons his trousers.

I get out the condom I have tucked in the pocket of my jeans, take it from its wrapper and get on the bed. I push off the comforter, for having had cleaned motels before, in now what seems like a former life, I know that they don't clean those and I do have my boys to worry about.

"And, for the hour?" He asks.

"Sixty," I tell him, over my shoulder, on all fours on the bed, still wrestling with the comforter.

"Nice ass, Ronnie," he says, behind me, "You've always had a nice ass."

"Thanks," I say, in the midst of rolling my eyes. He had been one of the more popular boys in my class. You know the ones, the ones that were groomed for success and managed to make it out of the town only to come back and take the town over and find out that their wife didn't want to fuck them anymore. A combination of John and all that Billy complained that I was but really wasn't. The type of boy that never gave me the time of day in High School, now he's paying me to fuck him.

Right.

I tell myself that the sixty will buy dinner tonight and a pack of cigarettes.

Before, that is, Billy takes the rest for his shit.

Just then, there's a knock at the door.

"You set me up?" I ask.

"Hell no, Ronnie," he tells me, "I like what we got going."

"Whatever," I tell him, sounding way too much like fucking Billy.

"Besides that," he adds, "I know you got shit going on. You about the only one not on fucking drugs. We all know you're trying to feed your kids. Why do you think you got such a long list of clients?"

"I don't have a fucking long list," I lie. Being told that the attractive part of me is the lack of drugs is no way to get me to blow you any better.

"And, you're good looking too," he adds, knowing he's got to grease something to get a little more, "Better looking than you were in High School."

Right, all I had to do was be in more pain than I was then. And, just think, at the time, after having had my first time having had been rape in High School, I didn't think being in more pain was possible. Until now.

Then, there's another knock.

"You're old lady come for you, finally," I tease him.

"No," he says, "She knows and is good with it."

"Right," I tell him, wondering what he had done to make her 'good with it.'

"Ignore it then," I tell him.

Then, there's another knock, followed by a yelling threat.

"Open the fucking door, Ronnie," a familiar voice yells. "Or, I'm busting it fucking down."

I look at my 'client,' he laughs, says, "You not me, apparently."

"Right," I say and get off the bed, placing the condom on the mattress. I tell myself that I have a spare and I'll throw that one out. No matter how well they clean, you never know.

As I cross the floor to the door, he says, "Does this go into my hour?"

"Shut the fuck up," I tell him and open the door.

Standing butt ass naked with the motel door open, I stand looking into the eyes of John. He's red faced and tears are in his eyes. He looks away from my nakedness and looks over his shoulders.

John tells me, "Get fucking dressed and get out here."

"I'm busy," I tell him. *My God save me from all of this, you were the only one that could and was willing to love me. Save me, please.* "I'm working."

Without looking at me, he says, "I'll pay you double. Get rid of him, reschedule if you want, just give me this hour."

"Double?" I ask. *My God I can't charge you and won't take your money. Just hold me, I don't know what's happened to me and where I'm heading. I need you, don't leave again. Please.*

"Double," he says, still not looking at me. "Just get fucking dressed and get out here."

I close the door and tell my client that I'll be back in an hour. When he objects, I ask what he was planning on doing after we were done, when he has no answer, I tell him:

"Right, then wait a fucking hour and I'll be back. You have the room for the day and I'm not staying here after we're fucking done. I'll be back."

I get dressed and walk outside.

John is standing by his car, smoking and crying.

"Ronnie," he says, "Why did you let me leave?"

"You're doing well?" I ask him. *Please tell me that everything is perfect for you and that you've found someone. Please tell me that I made the right decision and that you're dreams are coming true.*

"Not now," he says, looking down at my feet.

"You can look at me," I tell him. "I'm not on drugs, I'm trying to feed my kids, that's all. And, what the fuck does it matter anyway, you have your little groupies and I'm not getting fucked at home and he's on the shit that he's fucking so what does it matter?"

That's when he looks at me and says, "It matters to me."

And, inside I turn to jelly. I light a cigarette with shaking hands and attempt to cover myself like I'm still naked. Which in his eyes I am, clothed and all, as naked as I was the day we spent together in another motel room, so long ago and so far away. I turn away and feel my quirk rising up in me, the way it has every single time I've sold my time to another man, with his own lame story and sad excuses, with the woman at home just dealing with it or completely oblivious to the transaction.

"What happened?" John asks, after a long silence.

The question is uncomfortable, to say the least. So, in order to fight the uncomfortable feeling, I change the subject, get back to the matter at hand. And, I try my damnedest to blow him off completely by making him angry.

"You know," I tell him, glancing at my watch, "Time's a ticking."

"Right," he tells me, taking a drag and looking away, watching the cars go by on the highway for a minute before saying, "I forgot that you sell time now." He thinks a minute, watches more cars, and then says, "It's a shame that you don't have the past to sell, I'd like to buy that from you. You know, erase some of our stupid mistakes, and buy it all back, to prevent you from being this person, standing here, selling parts of you that I had to beg, bargain and steal from you just to show you that I care about you. That I, I . . ."

"Stop," I tell him. *Please don't tell me that you love me, please don't. If you do, I will fall to pieces at your feet and never be the same again. I will be nothing more than bits and pieces on the blacktop at your feet. There'll be nothing left of me, not even left of this person that I've knitted back together again, the wrong way. Not even of her. There'll just be nothing. Please, I beg of you, don't say it.*

"I love you, Ronnie," he says.

"And, you said it anyway," I say to myself, looking down, and take another shaking drag off of my cigarette. I'm instantly just mush, no defenses anymore, nothing but cracked pieces of my heart melted beneath his heat.

"Because that's how I feel," he tells me, adding, "I came back to tell you that, to get you and the kids and take you with me. Mike told me that Billy's been more hands on than he has before with you. And, it's either I take you and the boys with me or I fuck him up today. Your choice. But, I'm not leaving you in a motel room, selling your ass to feed the boys. Because, despite the fact that you are unusually thin, I know in my heart you're not doing drugs, just tell me you're not doing drugs."

"I did tell you already," I snap. "Besides that, what does it matter?"

"It matters to me," he tells me.

"God, you don't get it," I say, again, to myself, shaking my head and taking yet another shaking drag off the same cigarette.

"Then, tell me, then, Ronnie, please," John says.

Why do you have to fucking do that?

"Tell me, please, Ronnie," he presses.

I shake my head at him and open my mouth to speak, unsure of how to put it when I'm not completely sure of how to put it to myself.

"Just say it, Ronnie," he says, "No matter how bad it is, no matter what it is, you can tell me. I think I've proven that to you, haven't I?"

I shake my head and look away.

"Haven't I, Ronnie?"

"Yes, you have," I snap.

"Then, tell me, what is it?" He presses. "What the fuck happened?"

"You don't fucking get it," I snap at him and turn, like I'm going to walk away.

"Just don't leave," he tells me, adding, "Whatever I don't get, make me fucking get it. Make me get it, Ronnie, please. Don't go. I have the hour. I have the money. I'll pay you now. Just stay and make me fucking get it."

I stop and he tries to come closer, like he wants me to lean on him and it's too much, the place is threatening to spin and I am close to falling to pieces. I put up my hand and push him back a little, begging him with my stance, to give me a little distance.

"Make me get it, then, Ronnie," he tells me. "You know, you're right, I don't fucking understand. It's a matter of wanting to be with me and we go and get the boys and we're gone. Even if you change your mind once you're there, you can stay as long as you want and I'll take care of you. Of all people that need to be out of here, you do, out of here and away from him."

I shake my head and get angry and blurt out, "And, then, what?"

"Then, you're safe," he says, like it's supposed to be a given.

"I don't mean that," I tell him.

"What did you mean?" He asks.

I take a breath and close my eyes.

"Explain something to me," he begs.

"Fine," I tell him, adding, "Everyone has labels. My husband is an asshole, that's his label. But, if you look at why, he's then broken, damaged in some way or another. His thing that he's fucking is a prostitute, that's her label and her why is because she's a junkie, another label. But, what happens when you're not your label anymore?"

"When you change?" John asks.

"Yeah," I answer.

He laughs and shakes his head.

"Am I funny or just stupid?" I ask, adding, "Because I know I'm fucking stupid, you don't have to remind me of it and I'd appreciate not hearing it from you of all people."

"I'm not calling you stupid," he whispers.

"Then, why are you laughing?" I ask.

"Because we all change, Ronnie," he says.

"No," I tell him, "Not like this."

"What do you mean?" He asks. "You hooking? You won't have to, if you come with me. I'm not on drugs and I have money to take care of you and the boys."

"No," I tell him, "It's not that."

"Than what then?" John presses.

"What happens," I ask, slowly, unsure of even really wanting the answer, "When the damsel in distress isn't in distress anymore? Does she run back to danger because the knight."

"Her knight," he corrects me. *Oh, don't do that, don't fucking do that.*

"Fine," I correct myself, "Her knight is bored with no one to save and he goes looking for another damsel to rescue. What happens when her label is gone? And, she becomes something else? What does she become?"

He smiles and looks away, shaking his head.

I keep talking, trying to explain myself, "I mean I was mother and wife, I was dutiful daughter and obedient and good and it wasn't good enough and the label was taken from me and then I became damsel in distress, that's my label. What if I'm not even good enough for that label either? What happens when it's taken from me? Or, what if I give up the label altogether? What label replaces that?"

For a long moment, he looks at me, as I stand in uncomfortable silence, wanting nothing more than to curl up in his arms and forget the past few months with him gone. He just stands there, weighing me, watching, and choosing his words, one by one, before speaking.

I can't stand there, quietly, and keep talking, nervously.

"I was servant and caregiver," I go on, "I was hurt and shame and embarrassment and rejected. I've held so many labels that I just don't know anymore. I was pain, that's what my label was, just pain. Nothing I did was ever good enough for anyone. I've given and given, I've changed over and over again, transformed myself, been more than what was asked of me, given more than what was ever expected, and still I was pain. And, now you see me as damsel in distress, when I've put myself here and I can't expect someone else to admit their part in all of this, when I can't admit mine. What comes after damsel in distress? What label is going to come now? Am I even good enough to assume that I am a damsel in distress and not one of these stupid ass women out there getting wet off of getting beat and hurt and having that kind of attention? What label am I given if I give this one up? Is it guilty, because I am guilty of so many things? I guess I just don't understand. I don't get it."

For another long moment, he is silent, listening and weighing, judging, I'm so fearful that he's judging me and I'll be found wanting. He waits so long that I can't think and I can't concentrate and I'm throwing out one cigarette and lighting another just as quickly. By the time he answers, I'm on the verge of tears.

"I can give you a label," he says and looks away to the highway and back again, adding, "But, it's up to you if you want it or not, there's actually two labels, I'd like them to go together. But, it's up to you if you want it and if you can handle seeing and knowing that that label is yours."

"What is it?" I whisper.

"First," he says, "I'm amazed."

"Amazed?" I ask, saying out loud, my scattered thoughts, "I've been called many things and some of those on a daily basis and amazing or someone being amazed by me has never been one of them. So, knowing it's coming from you, I'm assuming it's a good thing?"

"It is," he says, explaining, "Of everything you've been through in the past few months and everything and all that you're being forced to do now, you have the sense about you to see your life in this way. I'm amazed. Completely blown away by you, you have no idea who you are and who you are to me."

I shake my head and look away to the highway and remember that he isn't supposed to stay. So, I attempt at redirecting his attention back to his dreams.

"I'm glad you left," I lie to him, adding, "How is the music career?"

"Don't do that," he says, adding, "It's my hour, I'm paying for it, and I know what you did, pushing me out the door because Mike told you to. I'll forgive you for that once, not twice. There are many things I will not do to you, because I could not do it to you, and you alone, please don't do that."

I take a drag off my cigarette and whisper, "Sorry."

"Right," he says, anger setting his face in stone as he looks away to the rooms behind me and adds, "Don't push me away again, especially for my supposed benefit."

"Sorry," I repeat, through choked voice.

He nods, looks away, lights another cigarette, and tells me, "The only label I want you to have is John's Ronnie. But, if you won't take that, just be Ronnie. Be yourself. Be you, wherever you are, and whomever you're with, be you and be safe and be true to you and those boys that's going to need you to show them what a real woman is so that they know who to seek and find and to hold onto. Be you. I would prefer John's Ronnie, but, I see so many labels that are hidden that I place on you every day."

"Like what?" I whisper.

"Like beautiful and blessed," he tells me, adding as I shake my head and look away, "like amazing and unbelievably strong and determined, like crushed and broken but not completely defeated. Because if you can ask a question like that in the midst of all of this nonsense, then, you aren't defeated. You're still fighting, tell me that you're still fighting."

I shake my head. *Don't fucking do this to me, please. Don't do this to me.*

"You don't believe any of it?" He asks.

"How can I?" I ask. "When all I've heard, before you showed up and since has been how ugly I am, how I'm not worth even the payment that the clients give me and he takes for his shit and for her so that she can get her fucking shit too. How can I?"

"Do you trust me?" He asks.

I shake my head and tell him, honestly, "I don't know. I don't know that I know how to anymore."

"Well, at least you've given to me that much," he says, adding, "I'll take it. I'll take it, happily. At least you've been honest about that and I'll take it."

I take a breath and go to send him away again, to redirect his attention to his dreams and far from me and my drama. When, all of a sudden, the motel room door opens and my latest client, the former classmate of both of us, comes outside, running his mouth about the time and about his time.

"I paid for time with her," he complains and pointing his finger and accusing John, "And, you fucking come along and I now have to fucking wait."

"Shut the fuck up," John tells him and turns back to me and says, "No more of this, Ronnie, please no more."

I don't know what to say.

The client continues, "I shouldn't have to fucking wait when I was the first fucking one in line. And, you show up and get bumped up in line and you're out here, doing fucking what? Talking to her? I got a fucking idea, you selfish prick, fucking call her later, once I'm done."

"I swear to God," John snarls at me, "I will fuck him up first."

"John, please don't," I tell him, out of energy to fight even myself.

"Come on, Ronnie," my client snarls, "We fucking doing this or not. I think I've waited fucking long enough, don't you?"

I don't know what to say.

"Back the fuck up," John tells him, taking a step between me and my client and completely loses it, "Go fucking home to your wife, who is stressed and ignored and who you're only with for her family's money and that cushioned job that they give you in their business office, like you could ever count without using your fucking fingers."

"You don't know what the hell you're talking about," my client tells him and then turns to me, demanding, "We doing this or not?"

I open my mouth to speak and John interrupts, continuing, "I got an idea, buddy, why don't you go find another one of your whores for the night and leave Ronnie to me?"

"What are you talking about?" My client snarls.

"What are you talking about?" I ask.

"He's fucked every one of them on the streets," John tells me, without turning to face me, standing toe to toe with the only way I'm going to feed my kids tonight. "Tell me you haven't," he dares him.

"No," my client says, and I can see that he's lying, "No, I haven't."

"He's lying," John says.

"I know that," I say, and shrug it off to my client and to where John doesn't see me.

"I haven't," my client says to me, begging me to come into the room.

"You have," John says, "I know you have."

"How do you know that?" My client asks.

"Yeah," I ask, "How do you know that?"

"Because," John explains, "There's drugs and prostitutes coming in and out of this place and I'm sure that the owners here don't want to lose their biggest clientele with all the attention that a scene would cause."

"Like this scene?" I ask.

"Yes," John answers, continuing, "And, they'd only risk it for certain people."

I turn and look toward the office, where, through the window I can see one of the owners nervously shuffling papers around.

I complete John's thought, "Only for a regular customer would you take the risk."

"Right," John says, "Spoken like the wise woman that's been forced to the streets.

My client looks to me and then to John and back to me again, and says, "I'll be in here waiting. Please don't take much longer."

I nod, numbly.

John turns around and starts pacing, talking to himself, "I've always fucking hated him. How many times have you fucked him already? You know something, don't fucking tell me, I'd like to think that I'm a better lay than he is, than he has ever been, I mean honestly, tell me it's just for the money."

I turn to tell him yes, to at least nod at him, and he's pacing around me and by his car, with his back to me, ignoring me and not knowing that it is about the money. And, if it were up to me, I'd be in bed with John every night, but, I'm not me anymore and maybe he should go back to his music, because I don't even feel alive anymore.

Before I can, though, John is off on another anger filled tangent.

"I mean, seriously, Ronnie, do you know how many fucking women he took advantage of in school? Just imagine all the street walkers, he's been doing this for fucking years. He's had every fucking last one of them and multiples of them. He alone has personally fed the heroin economy in this fucking town and now you. I was just getting to the point to where I was getting used to the idea of him fucking touching you after I left. I told myself, she has to survive and she'll have to fuck him, do anything for him, she has to do, I was just getting to that fucking POINT! AND NOW THIS! HIM! Why? Ronnie, my fucking God, why? You need money" he comes closer to me, standing over me, rubbing his lips against my forehead, "You come with me, numb yourself if you have to, I'll fuck you and pay you every fucking day."

I push him away, telling him, through tears, "You're not like that to me."

"You need money, don't you?" He steps closer again, "All you had to do was call and tell me and I'd be here, fucking paying you for it."

"YOU'RE NOT LIKE THAT TO ME!!!"

"But, he is," John says.

When he walks away, approaching his car, I ask, "Why are you doing this?"

"Making a raucous, causing a scene?" He asks, laughing, "I'm proving a point."

Just then, one of the owner's voices sounds from behind me, "You must go now. We don't want trouble. You keep yelling and causing loud cops will come. No one here wants cops to come."

John walks over, away from the car, standing in front of me, and addressing the owner, "Right," he glances at me and then back at the owner, asking, "You're just protecting one of your regular customers, right? Him, right? How often is he here?"

"Two, three times a week," the owner says.

"Right," John replies, looking at me again.

"You leave now," the owner repeats, "Or I call cops on you and you don't come back."

John laughs and walks back to his car, toward the trunk.

I turn, in his defense and tell the owner, "He's with me, he'll be leaving soon, okay?"

"He's with you?" The owner asks.

"He's with me," I tell him.

"If he's with you," the owner says, "I give him fifteen more minutes before I call." And, with that the owner walks away.

Before I could turn back, I hear John comment, "So, a regular customer too, are you? My fucking God, how often are you forced to be here?"

I close my eyes in shame, for the first time in over a month, I feel the old emotion, shame and it's like welcoming an old friend back into my circle. And, that feeling scares the shit out of me. When I open my eyes they're blurred from tears and I have to wipe them away to see clearly.

I turn around as John is yelling at himself, messing around in his trunk.

"What are you doing?" I ask.

He slams the trunk lid closed, a guitar in his hand. John walks over to me, stops just steps from me, takes one look at his guitar and smashes it on the blacktop before I can stop him or even figure out that that's what he's going to do. I scream, cover my mouth with both hands, and cry, as he smashes his beloved guitar to pieces and tosses the remnants aside, easily forgotten. He straightens his back, takes a minute, looking down at the smashed pieces, and wipes his hands on his jeans.

"Why did you do that?" I whisper, trying to calm the tears and wiping them from my eyes.

He takes a breath and looks over at me, saying, "You're more important to me than music. I can get another guitar. I can't get another you."

Don't fucking do this to me, please.

He walks over to his car, stepping over the damaged pieces, going to the driver's side, and comes back moments later, carrying a wad of cash.

He asks, "How much is he paying for an hour?" He asks without looking at me, ruffling the bills like he's counting them and his face red and tears dropping from his eyes.

"Sixty," I whisper.

"Right," he says, swallowing hard, counts out five twenties and hands them to me. I refuse, at first, to take them, cowering away from him. He takes my hands and puts the twenties into my hand and forces me to look him in the eye, closing my hand over the money.

John tells me, "Maybe for a night you won't have to do this. I want to take care of you and can. If this is your only option, the only one that's presented itself to you, call me and I'll come and fuck you and I'll pay you double every time. I promise. Just, for me, don't do this again, please, Ronnie, after today, don't. I'll pay you for that time, I'll pay double. I promise you." He brushes his lips against my forehead and whispers, "I am a man of my word."

With that, he turns and walks away.

John gets into his car and squeals angrily out of the parking lot and down the highway, toward his brother's restaurant.

"I know you are," I whisper.

Tears fall and I can't fight them, overly aware of the money in my hand. I stare at the guitar, and the pain returns with the shame, old friends come back to stay. I will never be another label deserving of whore and guilt and pain and shame. I know this now. I don't deserve John. I never have, not even that first day, so long ago. And, I certainly don't now.

But, I need him. I want to be with him. Don't leave again. Please, don't leave again.

Just then, my client steps out of the room and his voice brings me back to what I was doing, "Are you coming? Or, have I wasted all this time, waiting for you?"

I swallow hard, tuck the money in my jeans pocket and tell him, "No you haven't. I'm coming, give me a fucking minute."

"I've given you long enough," he demands.

I nod. And, I obey. Numbing myself again and turning around and going to the room, where I get to work and the anticipation makes the hour more like twenty minutes. And, he's gone, satisfied and I'm sixty dollars richer, for the moment. I don't count the one hundred twenty dollars from John. I can't and won't keep that money. Our time is free. Our time is precious to me.

Our stolen time is what has kept me functioning, as functioning as I am, still.

I take a minute in the parking lot and think. When I decide what I'm going to do, I start walking, toward Mike's pizza shop, down the highway, turning my back on the motel for another day. I have just enough time to drop off the money and watch his response, before going to the grocery store and getting home to get the boys off the school bus. So, I walk to Mike's pizza shop. Once there, I see John's car parked out front, I ignore it and go inside, asking one of the waitresses for Mike. When Mike does emerge from the back, from talking John down I imagine, I scribble a simple note on one of the receipts and hand the money and the note to Mike.

I tell him, "Give this to John, the note explains where I can't."

And, I walk away and out of the shop. Outside, I find a cluster of trees to hide within and watch. Several moments go by and John emerges from the pizza shop, toward his car when Mike stops him, handing him the money and the note. From the shadows I watch John's face, a tiny tear stained smile creeps across as he pushes the money into one of his pockets and reads the note. His lips are open in shock and more tears come.

I can't bear to watch anymore and emerge from the cluster to cross the highway and to the grocery store. There, I make sure to spend twelve dollars on a little bit of food, stuff like eggs and bread and oodles and noodles so that I have enough out of twenty for a pack of cigarettes, my only food for the night. The other forty, Billy will take for his fucking bundle, like he's taken the rest of the money I had made that day, either for himself or for her. I manage to get a cheap, discounted creamer, knowing that I had a little coffee left at home, and manage to buy them, too, a cheap snack of one whole dollar a box of off brand flavored crackers. With my purchases and my pack of cigarettes, I purchase after getting the food, I go outside, face the fact of having to then walk home again.

I count my change as I emerge from the store and realize that I can go back in and get them another box of crackers. I look up, just before turning back and see John standing there, by his car, waiting for me. There are tears in his eyes and he is eager to get my attention. No matter how badly I meant my little note. No matter how badly I want to hide in his arms, I can't. I am still prisoner to Billy and his wants. I am still a prisoner. If Billy sees anyone crossing the threshold of our home, any man that threatens his control, I'm done, jail or mental ward or worse. I swallow hard and step toward him.

"Did you understand my note?" I ask him, eyes to the ground at his feet.

"I do," he says, adding, "I just want to tell you first that I'm sorry for what I did earlier. And, Mike and I came up with this plan. I have pizzas in the back for the boys."

"I can never pay for those," I tell him.

"No one expects you to," he tells me, and when I try to object, he adds, "And, they're not a payment of anything, but, rather an apology for an overprotective brother who needs to mind his own fucking business and should have never told you to push me away. So, yeah, there's no charge, actually its payment to you. Do you understand?"

I look up at him and nod, fresh tears in my eyes.

"Thank you," I whisper.

I lean my head toward John and he steps forward, taking me into his arms and holding me as I cry. He kisses me on the forehead and on the top of my head, holding me like he never wants to let me go again. When he does, it's only to lead me to the passenger side and guiding me safely inside. He drives me home and I fight all the way to tell him that he can't come in, but, he won't let me speak, refusing to hear me push him away or give an excuse of why he can't take me home, why he can't come inside, why he can't deliver the pizzas on his own, and see Billy face to face.

He pulls up in front of my house and tells me, "Listen to me, I know you're working on trusting me, but, right now, follow my lead. Get out and go inside like nothing has happened. And, I'll bring the pizzas in for the boys. Just let me do all the talking. Even if you don't trust me yet, Ronnie, let me do this, for you. For us. Please."

I nod, get out of the car with my bags and walk to the front door, with John close behind, carrying the pizzas.

Inside, Billy sees me and immediately starts questioning, "What do you got for me? Because I have shit to get and shit to do and don't have time that you've already wasted in getting fucking money. I'm amazed anyone is willing to pay you."

And, on seeing John come into the house, Billy is immediately silenced. He stands form the dining room table and as I put the bags down on the breakfast bar, passes me, and murmurs in my ear, "Who the fuck is this? What's going on, Ronnie? Do you want to go away tonight?"

"Hi," John's voice interrupts the badgering, "I'm John, and I worked with Ronnie at the pizza place. My brother owns the shop and we just kept seeing Ronnie walking everywhere you know and my brother just thought that as a token of showing her how valuable she was as an employee and I think trying to get her to come back, you know, he sent me with these pizzas for the boys. You know, every kid likes pizza. Every boy does anyway."

Billy is instantly disarmed, not knowing what to say. He looks from me to John and back again. He finally, not knowing what the fuck to think, leans back against the sink, and crosses his arms.

"Did he now?" Billy asks. "Well, that was nice of him, thank him for me." He then turns to me and asks, "Do you have anything for me?"

I go to give him the money and John interrupts me by saying, "I got it Ronnie, you gave it to me to hold because you were afraid you were going to lose it." John takes out a wad of cash and gives it to Billy who promptly counts it: he's given him the five twenties which silences Billy and makes John his new friend. Billy's eyes dance with possibilities and within moments he is gone, leaving the house, driving off in the truck with the five twenties in his pocket and his blessing for John to be there.

"Why do you do that?" I ask John.

John laughs and tells me, "Because if I have to pay for your time and you won't take the money, I like the note by the way, we'll talk about that later, then I'll pay him to go away for a while. Would you accept that as a trade off?"

"Don't give him any money," I tell John, adding, "He's either going to give it to her for fucking or drugs for them both."

"Being able to be here," he tells me, "With you, is worth the loss and he's gone for a while, which is a good thing. Do you mind if I'm here?"

"No," I tell him. "I like that you're here. Why are you here? I mean in the past few months, I've been, well, you smashed the guitar and I don't want you to, why would you choose a whore over music?"

"I didn't," he tells me, clarifying, "I chose you. You're not a whore. You're Ronnie, a beautiful strong woman that's been abused, not a damsel in distress, but, a woman I love, a woman I can't get out of my head and my heart. I want you in my bed, in my space, in my life, nagging me, snoring next to me, if so be it, and I don't care, just as long as you're there."

I don't know what to say, and preoccupy myself with straightening the house and preparing for the boys to come home. When the bus is about to come, I stand out front and wave them in, shouting that they are coming home to a surprise, which makes them run faster to me and past me just as fast. They devour piece after piece and I cry knowing that it's because they've been on such a limited diet and I blame myself for failing to fulfill that need.

John waits until they have a mouthful and sits at the dining room table and invites them to sit with him. He talks to them both.

"My name is John," he explains, "I'm an old friend of your mom's and I think, I'm not really sure if either of you know, but, things have gotten a little uncomfortable here, lately, you think?"

My oldest, William, nods and says, through a mouth full of pizza, "We've noticed, but, mommy tries to hide things from us."

And, my youngest, Ron, interrupts and asks, directly, "Are we leaving yet? Are you here to take us away?"

John thinks a moment and glances up at me, tells them, "I'm here to do whatever your mother wants me to do. But, I'm here to let you know that I want to take care of all three of you. Can I have your support? You with me on this, I know you don't know me and it's right to be a little worried about who I am and if I will act the same way, but, I give you my word that I will not hurt any of you."

Will and Ron, all of nine and eight, look to one another, have an unspoken conversation, and Will asks John, "Will you take care of mommy?"

"That's your first question?" John asks.

"Yeah," Will says, shrugging.

My matter of fact son Ron, says, before Will can think of anything, "Well, yeah, because we know mommy will always take care of us, we're not worried about us."

"Yeah," Will agrees, "We're just worried about her."

John sits back, stunned, and looks up, telling me, "If you ever have doubted that you've done anything right, listening to your two boys in this time, should take that all away. They love you, too, Ronnie. I love your mom, guys, I do, and she doesn't think she's very loveable right now."

And, both of my boys get up from the table, forgetting their much needed food on the table, and walk over, wrapping their arms around me. Tears come and that's when it hits me. I've always done the right thing when it comes to them, now doing the right thing means repositioning ourselves. And, if I can't reposition myself first, I'll reposition them.

I wipe my tears away and get both of their attention.

I tell them, "Go to your room and get your old backpacks, one backpack a piece, and fill it with the toys and games you want to take and I'll pack the two of you a bag of clothes."

"Why?" John asks.

"Because," I say, still looking a long time into the eyes of my two wise little men, "You guys are going with John tonight, while I take care of what I need to take care of here."

Will and Ron look at me and at one another and then back at me again and simply nod before rushing to their room to pack their favorite toys and games.

"What are you doing, Ronnie?" John asks.

"You have to take them to Mike and Marie," I tell him. "Hide them. And, when they're gone, I can cut the chains and I'll follow after. I promise."

John sighs and looks down at his hands, saying, "I'm not leaving you here."

"You're not," I tell him, "You're taking the biggest and best parts of me with you. Please protect them and I'll be there soon. Do you trust me?"

"Do you trust me?" He asks.

"More than you know," I tell him, adding, "More than I thought I could."

He nods, looks around, tells me, "I'll be watching. I'm close, don't let him take you anywhere. Don't let him lock you in here."

I nod. And, leave the room, grabbing clothes for the two into two bags, a bag for each of my boys. And, gaging the time, I rush them out the door, each of them taking another slice of pizza with them. I pack them in John's car and tell both of them how much I love them. Then, I turn to John.

He says, "I'm not leaving you here, I'll be close."

I nod.

Before getting into the car, he asks, "Did you mean what you said in the note?"

"What did I say?" I tease.

He laughs, looks at the boys in the car, and then, back at me, "You said that our one day together is your hiding place, that that memory alone has helped you get through all of this."

"Did I say that?" I ask, innocently.

"Yeah, you did," he answers, adding, "Tell me you mean it and you'll never get rid of me."

"You may want to get rid of me," I tell him.

"No," he says, "After over twenty years I don't see that happening, do you?"

"I meant what I said," I tell him. "I'm not what I've been doing."

John grasps the back of my head and places a kiss on my forehead and then on my lips, cradling my face in his hands. He looks me in the eye and says, "I know that. I do know that. I can't replace you. I've spent twenty years trying, I'm not trying anymore. And, if all I have are your boys, that's more than I could have asked for. But, I want you. Promise me, promise me, you'll fight to get to me and you'll do whatever you can to reach me, to reach us. Promise me."

"I promise," I whisper, "Just take care of them. Protect them, please."

He nods, kisses me one last time, and gets into the car, driving away with the best things in my life. My heart in one car, past, present, and future. I wipe the tears, and set about coming up with a plan.

I've estimated the time correctly, because all I had was fifteen minutes to plan and act. He comes in, high, content, and I wonder how he's even able to drive the fuck home after that. And, yet, I wonder, too, how he's fucking her, and then I figure he's just buying her shit and the two of them are getting high together. Whatever the case may be, he's here and I have to do something quick.

And, still I don't know how to start.

Then, when he pauses in the dining room, surveys the scene, and asks a simple question, I know I've been given a door. And, I take, with my heart in my throat, I take the door and barge my way through.

For, he asks, "Where are the boys?"

Chapter 20

Gaining my freedom

Don't get into the truck with him.

And, yet how do I break free?

How do I gain my freedom?

I need him to be seen publically.

Somewhere else

Somewhere far from here

At least just outside of town

Don't trust what he says.

Don't listen to his reasoning.

Don't give into his anger.

They are your boys.

You're protecting them.

They are safe now.

They are safe.

Keep telling yourself that they are safe now.

And still you get into the truck

And still you go with him, lying about where they are

You're steering him out of town

You're leading him to one of your clients' house

You know where he lives, you went to him one day for extra

There, maybe someone else will see me

Maybe there someone else will stop him

Don't cry when he punches you.

Tell yourself that it's the drugs and nothing more.

Give him more excuses than you ever have before.

Just one more time, fill the excuses.

That way, you can release the two of you, once and for all.

Make peace with God

Please forgive me

Know that I did what I did because I had to

I had no other choice

My boys needed protecting

My boys needed me there, in their lives

Please, forgive me

I'm not angry at you God for anything

Please don't be angry with me

Keep the lie going.

You're almost there, another five minute drive.

You're almost there.

Then what do you do?

Steer the car into another car, a parked one.

Cause an accident.

Survive it or not, your boys will be safe.

They'll charge him here, out of town, out of state.

Almost there, judge the way you will cause the accident.

Gage how you will steer the wheel.

Cause an argument.

You'll get his attention and his fists.

Start an argument.

What about now?

Haven't we argued about everything at this point?

What is there left to argue about?

The boys aren't yours

You're right I am a whore

I have been fucking around on you from the very fucking beginning

They don't even belong to you

They belong to other men

Unknown men that paid me

How do you think I drifted so easily into hooking?

I've done it before dickhead

That's right, hit me.

Scream at me.

Get your attention off of the road and on me.

You hate me, right?

You want to kill me, right?

Keep it coming, just around the fucking corner.

There, just there, and that car, nice and big and just enough to stop us.

But, not large enough to cause that much damage to me.

Enough though to knock him out, hopefully.

Enough for me to gain someone's attention.

That's right, I'm a whore, you fucking asshole

You were the last man on earth I'd want near my boys

Stay away from me

Right, hit me again, another few feet.

NOW!!!

Chapter 21

The free girl

When you've locked up a girl for long enough, she will risk life and limb to break free, especially when she believes that she has ones that she loves worth protecting. She will lead you away and tear you apart. She will do anything and everything she can to break those chains in order to protect the ones she loves. And, the moment that those chains fall off, she will run and you will never see her again.

I wake in the street. People are gathering. My eyes concentrate on feet, many feet approaching, quickly. I push myself up and realize that there is pain from somewhere that I can't pinpoint, my head, my back, my arms, and the ache from where his fists have wailed into me reverberates through me. It feels as though he's still hitting me, still punching me and calling me names. Even his voice rings in my ears.

Hidden in the shadows, laying on the outskirts of the street, I manage to pick myself up and move to even darker shadows. I have to know that they see him, that they take him away, somewhere else, far from here. I have to know for myself, see for myself that he's gone. I scramble to nearby bushes and hide, or rather collapse. From my position, prostrate, on damp grass, I watch as the crowd swarm the truck and pull him out.

He's unconscious.

I sigh in relief and pull myself even further into the bushes. From there, I lay and wait. They call an ambulance and discuss among themselves that what if there were one than one passenger. I hold my breath and back up further, hiding myself. I haven't thought out the exact details of the entire plan, but, all I know is that I don't want to be found. Not yet. Not by any of them. And, somewhere deep inside, I'm hoping beyond hope that John has made it to Mike and Marie's, managed to drop off the boys, and is now wandering, looking for me.

But, he wouldn't know to look here.

I have to get back into town, I tell myself. I have to make it back, somewhere that John can find me. I have to make it back to my boys. Now, though, if I move at all, I'm done, I'll be seen and the questions will start and no one will believe me again. I have to stay hidden. I have to, I just can't be found. I pull myself even further back, out of sight and glance over my shoulder, to ensure that I'm not in someone's yard, you know, someone with the possibility of having a very large dog. I'm not in someone's yard, rather, I'm on the edge of the sidewalk, my back, as painful as it is I can't even feel the metal, is pinned against a wire fence.

I look around me. I can't stay here. Up ahead, is even darker shadows. If I can make it there, without being seen, I'll be alright. From there, I can start to backtrack and make it to the main road and maybe, just maybe be seen by John. For, he's the only one that will come for me, if he comes at all.

In the meantime, as I plan and try to figure out how to move to the darker shadows, I watch and listen as several paramedics and police officers come roaring into the street. When a police officer parks next to me, I close my eyes as though I were a child and under the belief that closing them will ensure my invisibility. Like I'm in this odd game of hide and go seek.

I need to get to that spot with the darker shadows.

It's almost as if the entire scene is one giant ball of light, too bright, despite how relatively dark it truly is, and the spot I desire is just on the other side of that ring, just up ahead, away from the crowd and the truck, the paramedics and the police officers. I inch my way, weaving through the bushes, pulling myself upwards, moving a few inches and freezing. The outer ring of light is so close after a while that I can nearly reach my hand to the darkness on the other side. But, there's this gap in the bushes, on the way there, that's exposed to light and completely void of even the thinnest of bush branches and brush.

I take a shaking breath and pray for a way, a door, anything, to get out of here.

And, just as fast as I can pray, my prayer is answered.

For, Billy stirs and wakes and starts fighting, swinging blindly at paramedics and police officer, onlooker and innocent bystander alike. He manages to take down an officer and two paramedics, demanding that bitch that he's married to, which makes me jump and back all the way against the fence until I threaten to bring attention to myself with the clang and bang of panic against chain. But, with all eyes on him, now is my chance and possibly the only one I may get.

I manage to sit up as he keeps swinging and hits a neighbor. I hold onto the fence and force myself to my feet, glancing every few seconds toward the scene to make sure I'm not noticed. It is then, standing and trying to find sure footing on two feet that I look up and he spots me.

"You fucking bitch," he screams and points, "I'm going to fucking kill you."

I grab my right leg that, at the time, refuses to move, and throw it into the darkness and plunge headfirst into the darkness after it. Just to stay unseen and unknown. And, I manage to fall headfirst unto pavement and scrape areas that are both bruised and unbruised, bringing tears to my eyes and a stinging to my face and hands. By the time I scramble to right myself and sit up, against a concrete wall in the dark, looking over to where he was standing and yelling at me, I see a sight that eases me and allows me to push onward and home.

They are restraining him and he's on the ground fighting them all the way.

Fucking drugs. Yet another promise left broken in our marriage. And, not the reason for his craziness, but, merely its accelerator. I lean my head back against the concrete and take a minute, taking in large shaking breaths until there are somewhat even. I then stand and head off away from the accident, limping and stopping when need be, but moving forward, away from the crowd. Some distance away, I realize that the one thing to the plan that I've forgotten is my hoodie. If only I had thought of bringing it, wearing it even, would have provided the extra cover by shielding my face from prying, curious eyes. Instead, for hours, I walk, and stop, sticking to the shadows and turning my head when passing anyone.

And, then, when daylight threatens to peak on the horizon, as the darkest of night transitions into the beginning of another day, I see up ahead, having stayed to side roads, in my slow motion, an unfenced yard, with laundry hanging on the line. And, there, among the pieces is a hoodie hanging to dry. I pray that it's dry by the time I get there. Sure enough, as I delicately pass and reach for it, it's dry enough. I remove it from the line, stumble and limp my way down further on the street and around the corner, where I put it on, lift the hood and breathe a sigh of relief that my face is hidden by the daylight to come.

And, soon, daylight is high and the blanket of darkness is gone.

I'm exhausted. I need to stop soon, but, I have to make it to daylight and figure out where I am first and how much further I have before stopping. Then, my legs give out and I'm forced to sit. I find a strip of concrete wall lining the sidewalk and there I prop myself up and shortly upon sitting, I fall asleep, hoodie hiding my face, my legs sprawled out before me, and completely ignored, like some other junkie that's just gotten high on the street.

Sometime, I wake with a start, with images of the crash flashing before my eyes and this paralyzing fear that Billy is close and looking for me and I have to run. When I wake, out of breath like I've run for miles, there's sweat in my face and the sun is high in the sky and blinding. I ease my way up the wall and, seeing the highway in the distance, I head toward the direction of the cars, and I'm assuming, is leaving the state and entering my hometown. The same hometown that knows everything horrific happening to me and never raises a finger to either stop it or aid in my safe passage.

But, my boys are there. John is there.

I make it to the highway, limping all the way and forcing one foot in front of the other. And, I tell myself that, despite the involuntary nap that I've taken, I really do have to stop. I have to rest, lay down on a bed, close my eyes, call someone from a safe place, and that's when I think that if I find a motel that I know, I can find a room. The past few months have made me a frequent, regular customer of many of the motels in the area. I'm sure to find one that I will find safety within for a little while.

I walk for a while longer, remembering the crash in more vivid detail than I would have liked, my quirk coming to haunt me again up close and personal. I need to stop. The quirk has become stronger, the more I walk, the weaker I am becoming physically. Now, it's taken on a life of its own, where my vision flashes in present time to the crash and back again, like a strobe light at full strength. It's making me dizzy and I'm beginning to lose all sense of where I am and what is truly happening.

I lean against a large boulder on the side of the road and this parking lot that opens to an unseen business of some sort or other and it takes several moments before I remember. I look down, feel the boulder, and focus on its smallest crevices.

"I know you," I tell the boulder, laughing. "I sat on you one day, waiting for a client that, at the time, I was sure was a cop. But, turned out he just had a tiny dick and a very angry wife."

That's when I laugh. I sit down on the boulder and laugh. It takes all of this and that stupid fucking boulder to make me laugh about the hole that I've fallen into. A hole that I thought was never ending, when, in truth, stopped short and with me laying at the bottom sure that this was it and there was nothing else for me or anything. It takes this to make me fucking laugh about my recent past and make peace with it, truly.

The sound of my cackle, as soothing and as healing as it may be, scares the other pedestrians far from me, and they nearly jump off the sidewalk to get away from me. The sight of their quick movements away from me makes me laugh harder. What little they know of monsters and evil. What little they know of surviving to see the sun again and to breathe fresh air when even you are betting against yourself. I laugh and release so much with that laughter. And, the quirk eases and crawls back into its bunk in my head, for a moment or two.

And, that's when I remember what the business is that the boulder sat before.

A motel.

A very familiar motel.

I smile to myself and force myself back to my feet and manage to limp across the parking lot to the main office. There, I wait until all the traffic has dissipated and the familiar owner is alone behind the desk to approach.

I take a shaky step forward, lift my head enough to reveal my identity and tell him, "I need a room, fucker."

"Quick stay or hour or so?" He asks.

"Waiting list today, then?" I ask.

"Longer than it's been," he says. "You have money?"

I am about to make an excuse and just get a room for an hour or so and then I remember I do have money, a little money and I manage to find it still in my pocket, untouched, and unmoved, despite all that has happened in the past 24 hours. I find it, smiling.

"Thank you, John," I tell myself.

"They all John," he says, asking, "How much?"

"I have forty," I tell him.

"Two hours," he says, "I give you two hours."

I nod, give him the money and take the key. Before leaving, though, I have to ask what the room number is, since for some unknown reason to me at this point, my vision is blurred. He tells me the number and I set off, out of the office and in search of my room. Oddly enough, it's the first room I had ever got at this motel. Now, I'm back, sure it would be my last.

But, at least, I tell myself, I'm at peace.

I find the room and manage, finally, with key fumbling in the lock, to open the door and lock it behind me. There, I ignore the bed, head off to the bathroom and a possible shower, hoping to get to the bottom of how bad I look and what the exact damage is at this point. So, ignoring all mirrors, I go to the tiny bathroom and strip down to nothing and turn to face the full length mirror. No words. There are no words.

I'm bruised on my arms and legs, large circular bruises where his angry fists attacked. There's other bruises that I guess is from the actual impact from the way I was sitting in the truck when we hit the parked car. Some of these are on my face. But, the two black eyes are apparent and I'm wondering if I have a broken rib or two from the pain that I realize now had been related to breathing, not moving. My face and my neck and one of my arms are scraped and raw from having had landed face first on the pavement when I dove for the shadows. And, there's a tiny gash on my forehead. The dried blood makes me feel better but still has me worried, not knowing where this came from either.

I turn on the shower, as hot as I can possibly make it and being able to withstand and step within its penetrating pulse. The water is shocking and stings in areas it normally wouldn't, but, it quickly numbs and relaxes like nothing else. I stand under its rush until the heat is gone and I turn off the flow and get out, gingerly drying myself with the miniature towels provided. I put my clothes back on and leave the bathroom, leaving the light on because it's always made me feel safe to do so.

I stumble to the bed, put my hoodie back over my head and lay in the most comfortable spot I can find, on my right side, facing the window. I still have this fear that Billy will come and find me, and that he'll come looking and no one will redirect him, no one will send him away. And, then, I worry that he'll find the boys or that that little fucking junkie is rooting through my house right now, stealing what shit she can sell to get more of her shit or just for the hell of it.

And, then, this memory appears, a soft soothing memory that I only would use on those rare moments when the pain was so intense I needed something to redirect me, to soothe me, and to ease the horror. It is a memory of John and that afternoon we spent together in another motel room. He had just taken his time, made love to me, and wrapped his arms around me as I dozed slightly. He was running his hands through my hair and humming a sweet, sweet lullaby to me to ease me into sleep. He did this thinking that the pain I was feeling then was because of Billy when it was really because I knew I was losing him. Nonetheless, it was a soothing moment and a rarity in my life, especially as of late.

I think of that moment, now, so much so, that I can nearly feel his hands through my hair, his arms around me and that soothing lullaby hummed in my ear. I relax and manage to close my eyes, and I sleep. When I wake, it's dark. And, I wonder why no one has come for me. Usually, if you stay too long, they knock and then send a cop. Maybe, he's given me more time for all the rooms that I paid, out of pocket, for the full day and only used for a portion of time. Then, I remind myself that he is who he is and he is more concerned with money than anything else. And, at the moment, I am too comfortable, too relaxed to even attempt at moving. I have no movement left within me and refuse, simply refuse to worry about anyone coming for me to remove me from this place.

Rather, I close my eyes again, to the hum and the hand through my hair and his arms around me, holding me tight. Sometime later, I hear voices and then footsteps. And, I'm sure they've sent the cops to remove me.

"Please don't arrest me," I murmur.

And, rather than angry hands or a demanding voice gaining my attention to leave, I hear a familiar warm peaceful voice and the gentle hands to match, slowly pulling my hoodie away from my eyes.

"I'm here, baby," John says. "I'm here."

"Am I alive?" I ask.

"Absolutely," he says, and I can hear the gratefulness and the tears in his voice. He adds before turning away, "You're not going anywhere. I know you think you've come here to die, but, you're wrong. You're not dying today or any day soon. I'm not letting you go now."

"John?" I ask. "The boys?"

His smile lightens me as he tells me, "They're safe, they're good. They're overly fed and being spoiled as we speak."

"Thank you," I tell him.

He reaches forward to take my face in his hands and I wince away from him.

"You don't have to be afraid of me, babe," he whispers to me. "You should know that I won't hurt you, I'd never hurt you."

"It's not that," I tell him.

"Then, what is it?" He asks.

"You don't want to see me," I tell him.

"I do," he says, and removes my hoodie from my face. I hazard a look in his eyes, forcing myself to deal with the rejection now, rather than later, once the pity is all gone. Instead, I find not rejection but anger and pain. "I'm going to fucking kill him."

"Do you still want me?" I ask him.

He stands and looks to the room around him, to figures I imagine are standing around, out of my eyesight. He tells them to bring the car around to the front, close to the door, so that they can get me out without anyone's interference or questions.

On their way out the door, he tells them, "Give us a minute, please."

"Anything, John," they tell him and leave.

He crawls into bed next to me, laying his head on the pillow facing me, and makes sure to keep his eyes on mine. He gently pulls the hoodie away from my face and off my head completely and takes his fingers and slowly and gently touches every scar and every bruise, every raw spot and every mark. He runs his fingers over my black eyes, gentle enough to be close but without the pain of pressure.

John then says, "You did this to get to me, to get to your boys. You did this to protect the ones you love. I find that beautiful and honorable and right now, I want to spend the next thirty or more years, whatever God is willing to give to the two of us, loving away all memory of every bruise and scar, every scrape and every word spoken associated with them. You have no idea what I want to do to you, to do to protect you and to ease your pain. I love you, Ronnie, more than you'll ever truly realize."

Tears well up in my eyes, as he continues to touch the bruises and scrapes and memories. He continues this loving motion for some time and tears flow easily now, I'm relaxed and at ease, and able to give to him this release of pain. The same thing I'd been hiding from everyone, for Billy hated it when I cried, now John gently pries the pain from me to get to the peacefulness.

"What are you thinking?" He whispers.

"That it's not about your words," I tell him, "It's what you can show, it's what you back up in all that you say. You just don't say, you do. I can never repay you for all that you've done for me."

He kisses me on the forehead and the other guys return. They offer to carry me to the car. But, John refuses to let them.

"I wouldn't even trust you guys with this cargo," he tells them and lifts me from the bed, carrying me to the car, where he places me in the backseat and gets in after me. Then, he lifts me back into his arms and has one of the other guys drive us.

On the way, he talks to me.

"Where you have had no family, I've brought you one. This is my band. Eddie is driving, he's my drummer. That's Joey in the passenger seat, he's on bass and guitar and sings and writes and is very flirtatious. He is only allowed near you in my presence." With that, the guys laugh and tease Joey. "And, next to you, behind you, is G man, don't ask, it's a long story."

They all laugh and the sounds of their conversation, like brothers coming together that have known one another all their lives and I've missed all that has come before. It feels like you've opened a book to the 20th chapter and you have no idea what's come before. I smile to myself and nudge myself into his shoulder. By the time we reach our destination, the pain is too much and I'm crying and whining and moaning and trying to find a comfortable position to lay.

"What's the matter with her?" One of the guys ask.

"She's in a lot of pain," John explains. He leans to me and whispers, "We're almost there. Is there anything I can do?"

I shake my head no and move my back a little to ease the pain. Nothing works.

My face feels raw and on fire. Every spot where he has punched and left his mark aches. My back and legs burn, there's shooting pain through my arms and my chest. With every breath there's a throb in my side and my head pounds. I can't get away from the pain. This, though, is worse than the inner pain that you can't reach, caught in an invisible box somewhere that screams out until your thoughts are drenched in the noise.

This, this is too much.

"Please," I beg.

"We're here, honey, hold on," John whispers as the car stops and the engine is silenced.

With tear filled eyes closed against the cruelty of light and sound, I'm lifted and carried from the car, through a yard and into a house, where a barrage of voices discuss how awful I look and ask what has happened. John abbreviates the story into quick commands and short phrases of explanation. He's told by a familiar voice that a doctor is waiting in the bedroom. Up the stairs, I'm carried and down a small hallway to a tiny room, where I'm placed on a soft cold mattress.

I manage, there, to find a comfortable position and then the doctor comes in and it all starts again. Hands are on me, my clothes removed, I even can swear I could hear a phone snapping photographs of me. In and out of consciousness, I see the doctor, his face up close, and at one point John is angry and in tears and leaves the room. Then, he's back and the doctor presses a cold gloved hand against my side, finding the rib I thought was broken. I scream out in pain and reach out and punch him. Then, hands are holding me down and my vision is blurred and the ceiling in the room is pink, this dull pale pink that only a young prepubescent girl would choose for her room.

And, John's lips are close and his voice is in my ear as my chest is wrapped, "Listen to the sound of my voice. Concentrate on the words, don't worry about the pain. Sometimes we have to go through pain to get to the healing. But, you're not going through this alone anymore. I'm here, honey, and wherever I go, you go with me."

The ceiling is comforting. The words are soothing. The pain grows. And, then there's this needle and a warm feeling and peace. I hear myself sigh and sleep drags me, wrapped in a warm blanket and there's no pain. And, the voices in the room slowly go far away, discussing how I need to sleep and rest and heal a little and the boys are safe and need to not see me until I'm not in pain anymore.

And, I hear myself mumble, "When will that be?"

And, a voice answers, from somewhere out of reach, "Soon, the pain will all be gone, honey. Soon. Sleep now. I'm not going anywhere."

I allow sleep to take me, obediently.

Chapter 22

In and out and in between

For someone not accustomed to pain medicine or any kind of medicine it hits hard.

Once it's given, it's strong and holds on for some time.

I wake and see flowers, the brightest most joyous colored pedals drooping nearby.

Close your eyes

Rest now

All is well and all is peaceful here

Sleep

I wake again with dark shadows dancing in the room.

The sound of dishes and laughter from somewhere beyond these walls.

A shadowed figure dozes in a chair by my bedside.

I smile and the movement brings pain and tears and moans.

The figure leaves and returns.

My head is lifted, medicine in mouth, and a drink of cold liberating water.

And, no pain.

Sleep now

Rest

Enjoy the peacefulness

Flowers, fields of them

Soft music of dishes and laughter

A humming from somewhere

Arms around me and humming in my ear

That sweet soft lullaby

Waking with arms around me.

Curling up closer and drifting back off to sleep.

Waking with light streaming in through the window, bright and cheerful.

Drifting back off to the sound of an acoustic guitar playing.

Then, opening my eyes to a wondrous sight.

Peaceful, sleeping, aged face laying on the pillow next to me.

One hand in my hair and his other on my hip.

I watch him sleep for a moment, maybe more.

Then, I place my hand on the side of his face and lean in and press my lips against his.

There is pain now, but, only a dull ache.

When my lips touch his, he wakes with a start.

Are you alright

Yes

Pain

I'm alright

Good

How good

Wonderful

I like that word

Me too

I smile, run my hands down his arm to his hand, still resting on my hip.

I look back at him with a seductive look.

No

You don't want me

I don't want to hurt you

You won't

I'm afraid I will

You won't

But I'm afraid I will

And the quirk appears just as there's a knock at the door.

Chapter 23

The damaged girl

The damaged girl can heal and be whole again, in theory. But the memory of her past will always be there, like another person in the room. The damaged girl can find love again, in theory. But the cracks will show and the weak spots may never be as strong as they should be and when she realizes this, if she realizes this, there is a tendency to run away and hide. For, when the structure reveals cracks and weaknesses, the owner leans toward abandoning the structure and looking for a stronger one, solid and undamaged.

The damaged girl can heal and be whole again, in theory. But she will never see herself the same way in the mirror again. And, this will affect the way she interacts with others, the way she holds herself and the decisions she makes from then on. The damaged girl can move on and grow, but the growth may be stunted and the movement labored and slow, at best. For, every step will be marred by worry and every movement toward improvement will be tinged by the memory of the past.

How can you ever truly move on then?

John leaves the room and I struggle to sit up, on the edge of the bed, fighting the pounding in my head and searching the room for a cigarette. When John returns, he sees me sitting again, and asks how I'm feeling.

"Do you have a cigarette?" I ask, not looking at him.

He hands me his pack, over half full with cigarettes yet to be touched, and gently smooths my hair before leaving the room again. I light one and relish the feel of that first drag. And, the quirk continues, as though knocking on the door for entry. Having had nothing to eat in I don't know how many days, I'm too weak to fight it and succumb to memories better left ignored and buried deep in the ocean depths.

I cry and can't control my breathing. My heart pounds in my ears and my chest feels as though it's going to explode. My hands shake, more and more with every movement of cigarette to mouth and back again. And, the room, the smoke, and even my clothes feel constricting and close and suffocating all at once.

With the lack of food and my head pounding and my body still weak, I am forced to ride the wave, waiting for the storm to end yet again. I fight beliefs of inadequacy, worries of Billy finding me, John being a monster in disguise, and feeling as though he has just rejected me, which leads me to question and over analyze every single moment we've shared thus far. My fight or flight switch is malfunctioned and has been this way for over twenty years. I am accustomed to this, and yet, in moments when I've been forced to fight for so long and I'm weary and just don't want to fight anymore, I would like to know the feeling of comfort without worry, without this quirk appearing and refusing to go until the wave has ended and the storm has calmed.

I hate this.

I want to know how it feels to be normal and unbroken, complete and undamaged. And, yet, here I am, with the cards I've been dealt and once again I'm waiting. I'm either waiting on freedom, waiting on acceptance, or waiting on peacefulness. I'm tired of waiting, of fighting, of dealing with this nonsense, and of being this broken, fucking damaged thing that is weak and at the mercy of the life's elements.

I stand, angrily, and go into the tiny room off of the bedroom that I was hoping was a bathroom and revealed to be, thankfully. There, I use the bathroom and fight my emotion imbalance and my weakened limbs into the shower, where I cry and angrily fight myself. When it seems that the worse of the storm is over, and the hot water nearly gone, I get out and find clean clothes, mine, neatly folded on the bathroom sink. I smile, dry off, and get dressed. Back in the bedroom, I sit down, light up a cigarette and find a steaming hot cup of coffee and a plate of food sitting on the bedside table.

I smoke, drink the cup of coffee, and eat. These little, seemingly, everyday things helps me balance my thoughts and my emotions to the point to where I can think clearly again and at least feel a degree of normal. I'm sore, now, but the ache is dull and the pain is nearly gone.

After another cigarette, and seeing that John hasn't returned, I go downstairs and wander the house a little, looking for anyone. The house is empty. The only hint of anyone having even been there is a fresh pot of coffee on and a half burnt candle still flickering on the dining room table.

It's not a large house, but, larger than mine. It's not lavishly furnished, but, you can tell that there was a degree of money involved, at least a little money, here and there. The kitchen seems newly decorated, as does the living room and the dining room. The one room that strikes me as odd and makes me wonder about its owner is the music room. An old upright piano stands in the corner, against one wall, an array of guitars, both acoustic and electric, that seem to be lovingly used and maintained rests in their stands amid microphones, amps, and recording equipment. And, decorated throughout are photographs of the band, press releases, open notebooks of lyrics, framed club openings, and reviews.

I read some of the lyrics and am intrigued, wanting to hear the recording of some of them, any of them. I search the room and kick myself for knowing nothing about recording equipment or how to playback anything and find, the only thing out of place in the room, a cellphone, sitting idle.

I look around, feeling uneasy, and still seeing no one, turn the phone on and swipe the screensaver. It immediately goes to a screen of a recorded video. I push play. It's a video of John and his band, playing a song in this room. The song is beautiful. I listen and watch and have to sit, blinking away the tears constantly. John's voice is haunting in the song and with the sweetness of the acoustic guitar, it's a heartbreaking song of loving a damaged woman.

Loving me.

I know you're broken

Bruised, bleeding and scared

I know you've been walking

That line between right and survive

I know you're looking

For a way out anywhere

And, I know you're worried

That you'll never feel alive

I can pay for an hour or more

For a lifetime of smiles

In a room without doors

I can pay for every moment you find

For a lifetime of miles

I'll carry you this time

You don't have to do this anymore

You'll be safe with me tonight

I know you're damaged

Crushed and broken in two

I know you're wandering

Through life's comedy

I know you've been selling

What's been taken from you

I know you're worried

That you'll never be free

I can pay for an hour or more

For a lifetime of peace

In a town without whores

I can pay for every moment you find

For a lifetime of needs

I'll even pay double if you'd like

You don't have to do this anymore

You'll be safe with me tonight

He's forced your hand

Kept you chained to him alright

Filling his every demand

Believing his lies

He's scarred you and marred you

Broke you in flight

Don't wander the streets of this town

Come be with me tonight

You don't have to do this anymore

You'll be safe with me tonight

You'll be safe, you'll be safe with me tonight

I listen and watch and listen again, watching the video over and over again. He's written a song about me. I can't believe that anyone would even consider me good enough to give me time or space, to take care of me, and to, of all things, write a song about me.

I place the phone back down and go back to the room. There, I think for a long time. I need to see my boys. I need to do so many things. I need to figure this all out. I can't sit here and believe that I need to be rescued and allow the rescuing without fixing myself in the meantime. I need healing and can't expect John or any other man to heal me. I have to do that on my own, for myself.

But, what do I do?

What can I do?

I go to the bathroom and look into the mirror. My face is bruised, and the bruises are turning a sickening yellow now, less black, but, just this sickening color. I no longer look scary, at least I don't think that I do. But, to a child, especially to two boys worried for their mother, I'm not sure.

I find my shoes and leave the house, taking several moments to figure out where I am. The house is still in town, just on the other side and I'm sure that Mike and Marie are nearby. Not sure, I call the pizza shop and ask. Sure enough, they live around the corner. Two minutes, I'm there, standing on the corner, watching, unable to approach the house, hidden beneath the hood of my hoodie, and just unable to move. The boys are playing in the yard and laughing and enjoying themselves.

I'm the least of all their worries and, as heartbreaking as it is, I like that.

I like that they aren't worried about me.

I spend hours watching them, sitting on the curb, under a tree, and smoking. While sitting there, I think and think and think. I contemplate giving custody of them to Mike and Marie and just vanishing until I can get better, because sitting there, I realize just how sick I am. The quirk isn't a quirk, its anxiety attacks. And, I have to face the fact that I am sick and need help. I need a therapist and a psychiatrist and medication. I'm broken and I've been pretending that I've been fine for far too long. When I've been on the verge of falling down so low that no one will be able to find me again. I decide, then, coming to this realization, that that's the first thing I have to do.

Then, I think about Billy. Filing for divorce is the least that I have to do now. Billy hasn't deserved the time that I've invested. And, he certainly hasn't deserved the time that I've stayed married to him. I am not sure that I deserve anything more than what I had with him, but, I do know that after everything, filing is what needs to be done. Now.

Then, I think about the house and getting back there to make sure everything is okay. I wonder if I have anything left. With Billy's junkie, I'm sure, running in and out and selling everything she can get her hands on, I doubt there is anything left, at least of any value. But, what is more valuable? Electronics or pictures of the boys? What has more of a value? Their favorite blankets as babies? Or, televisions and game systems that I can replace? In order to save those precious things, though, I have to get there and secure the house and everything in it, pick through the leftovers if need be.

With a list this long of what I have to do, I'm not sure of where to start. But, I have to. There is only so much that I can expect, allow even, John to do on his own and for me. I have to take over the little details. I have to fix this here. Fix me. I have to and not rely on someone else to tell me what to do and how to do or even expect them to do it for me. I've been claiming, all this time, that I'm not one of those women, when in fact I have been, allowing men to control everything in my life and changing to suit their likes. It's time to be what I've claimed to be all along. It's time to stand on my own two feet and finally find the strength to be myself.

I tell myself, let's change our own label and fight to keep it.

I can't expect John to take on the three of us, all like children to be cared for. And, I want to give to him more. He deserves more. He does. More than me, the me right now, he deserves more than this. I love him, I do. But, I can't love him, not the way that he deserves, and certainly not the way that I know I can.

I have to do this. For my boys. For myself. And, for John, to be with him.

I decide, sitting there, just then, after hours of watching the boys and laughing and enjoying their happiness. After hours of thinking about what I need to do, I decide, first, the priority of the list, rearranging a few things, and prioritizing the way I should have done months ago, rather than allowing Billy to hold me down and push me further into the hole I'm now struggling to get out of. And, I decide, that after this cigarette I will do the first thing I've placed on the list.

It is then, the moment, as life takes one last laugh at me, that I put out my cigarette and stand to leave, that one of my former regular clients pulls up next to me and calls me over. It is at that moment that I realize that I've left something off of that list: money. And, as I walk over to the car, I am tempted to get inside and just go make a quick sixty dollars toward the money I know that I need.

I walk over the car, to the driver's side door, the window down and my former client smiling in surprise. He's an older man, gray at his temples, overweight and has been a prostitute loving widow for years. I nod and wait for the obligatory proposition.

"My God, Ronnie," he says, smiling, "Where have you been? I've been looking all over the place for you. Why don't you get in and you can make some money and we'll both be happy for the day?"

I stand there and think. The memory of John's arms around me, of him talking to my boys, of my boys laughing and smiling and happy, the fact that they knew all along what I was going through, despite the fact that I was trying my damnedest to hide it from them, and of that song. I look over my shoulder and can still see the boys laughing and playing and then I survey my surroundings. I feel different. I look different. And, I realize, standing there, that I look horrible and for someone wanting to pay me for a lay, he didn't even ask if I was alright. I think, and I know it's awful to even admit this, that this last tidbit cemented my decision. I could argue for the good of why I need to do this, the boys need money, I need money for them, and I need to help John, to stand on my own, and I need money to do this. But, no, it was the fact that this potential client, a regular didn't even ask if I was alright, that simple fact that I couldn't argue away.

I back up from the car and shake my head, telling him, "Not today, have a good one and I hope you get lucky." I light a cigarette and walk away from his stunned expression.

By the time I get to the house, I've turned down a total of three such offers. And, it's with the last offer that I realize just how far I had fallen down that hole. I had so many regular clients that I didn't even remember the last one at all. And, yet, he knew me and knew details of me that few others knew, at least I thought there had been few.

I am ashamed as I turn the corner and approach home. And, the closer I get to the door, I realize what I thought had happened has. Shame quickly turns to something of a combination of irritation and anger. The door is open and when I approach, I can hear someone rummaging through the house inside.

I open the screen door and enter. I wait. Nothing happens. No one approaches. No one emerges. Yet. I take several steps, stepping from the breeze way to the kitchen, pausing in the center of the kitchen and listen. The rummaging continues in another room in the house. I take several steps and attempt to figure out which room and who it truly is that is there. Billy's junkie could have sent anyone. And, it could be any of his junkie prostitutes or someone he owes money to.

Be cautious, I tell myself.

I cross the rest of the length of the kitchen and look around the corner, straining to hear from which room the sound of rummaging is coming from. After several moments, I estimate that the direction it's coming from is Billy's room. Or, rather, our bedroom. I take my next steps cautiously, creeping through the living room and down the hall and peering around the corner into our room before entering. There, a young girl, maybe barely twenty, is rummaging through the safe, looking for anything valuable. All she has found is papers: birth certificates, marriage certificate, memories of times passed, and no money, nothing of value.

But, it is not Billy's junkie.

I step into the room, making sure she's alone.

And, I say, "Wow, you're a new one, I don't know you."

She freezes, looks up slowly, and around, looking at me over her shoulder.

"Who are you?" She asks.

"Stand up and face me and I'll answer whatever questions I feel like asking," I tell her.

She laughs to herself and stands, facing me, saying, "Wow, you're fucking cocky for someone that's breaking and entering."

"Wrong," I tell her. "I live here, you do not."

With that, the smile vanishes from her face and her face goes pale.

"You're the wife," she says, adding, "We were sure you were dead."

"Not dead," I tell her. "But, you on the other hand, I'm not sure how much time you've got."

She looks around and surveys her options.

One thing confuses me though and I ask, "Who is this we you mentioned?"

She straightens a little, not looking like a junkie at all, probably a pill head, I tell myself, or just some damn prostitute he's claimed, "Billy sent me to find something for him and I can't find it. Maybe you can help me."

"Why the hell would I do that?" I ask.

"Because he has your boys," she says.

Knowing where my boys are, and knowing he doesn't have them, I don't react, thinking, that by telling her that's a lie would mean that he would know that I know where they are and by getting to me, he can find them. So, I fake a reaction, telling her, "What do you need help finding?"

She nods, saying, "You don't know where they are either, then. Well, he'll be pleased with that one. At least he can work through the state to get them back. No one's going to give them back to a prostitute mother like you."

I was right. She was playing me for information. If I hadn't gotten that, the boys would certainly be in danger. And, I would have to be looking over my shoulder constantly. For, I wouldn't put it past Billy to send anyone after to me in order to find them.

"I need to find court papers," she says, sounding confused.

I roll my eyes, think that that's what he's trying to do, get the courts to flush me out or remove his junkie from his life completely. Either way, it's an attempt at a last straw. I roll my eyes and point to this cubby hole next to his side of the bed.

"Over there," I tell her, adding, "He hides his secrets either in his phone or in that cubby by the bed. I'm sure that that's where they are."

She nods, searches the spot and comes out with the papers. As she stands, she tells me, "Thank you. You're not as bad as he says you are. I guess I don't have to live with you, though."

"Right," I say, and move aside to let her out of the room.

I follow her through the house and watch her leave. Once she's gone, I take a seat at the dining room table and gage the damage done to the house. The televisions are all gone. The game systems too, I see from my seat, are gone. They've stolen from my boys. But, I knew that they would. I knew. The computer is gone and some of the appliances and a few other things, like DVDs and Blu rays and the games the boys didn't take with them. The microwave, toaster oven, coffee pot, and even the toaster is gone. It's a wonder they haven't taken the refrigerator. I'm sure if they could have taken it out the door, they would have.

My hometown and they've been silent witnesses to my ongoing defeats.

And, now they've watched as others have stripped our lives of all that we have.

This isn't home. This truly has been a prison, but, the prison walls extend to outside of these walls. This entire fucking town is like a prison.

I have to get the boys out of here, out of this fucking town, and not look back.

I look around at the walls and what's left in my home. There are so many memories in this house, both good and bad. I realize sitting there that monsters come into your life and stay by giving you the crumbs of kindness. They give enough to have you trained in begging for more. While, from the table, they're dining with strangers that they're giving everything to.

That's how the past ten years of my life has been spent.

And, even longer. My entire life has been spent this way, accepting crumbs when I could have feasted at the table. I have to figure out what I'm taking and how and where the boys and I are going. I can't live without them and won't, not now, I'll fight to keep them if I have to, but, I won't give them to anyone. But, I have to figure out where we're going.

In order to do that, I need money. And, there's nothing of value left in the house to sell, thanks to Billy and his junkie and their habits. For a moment, sitting there, I kick myself in the ass for not taking the offers as they had presented themselves just moments before. I could have made nearly two hundred dollars in a few hours. Two hundred dollars is a hell of a lot better than the nothing I'm looking at.

I rest my head in my hands and sigh, at a loss. I will have to lock up the house, complete my list and go back to the house from where I have been healing, the house I'm sure now belongs to John. There, figure out where we are going and to figure out where I can stand on my own two feet and rebuild in order to give the boys and John more than what they have of me now.

Just then, the screen door opens causing me to nearly jump out of my skin.

I turn quickly to see none other than John walking in through my door.

"I thought you'd be here," he says.

I sigh in relief, nod and tell him, "Yeah, I wanted to see what they left. Not much but I expected that."

"I'm glad you were expecting it," he says, walking through the kitchen and taking a seat next to me at the dining room table. "I knew days ago and was afraid of how to tell you."

"Yeah, I knew," I tell him, adding, "How long was I out?"

"About a week," he says, adding, "Give or take five days."

"Nearly two weeks?" I ask, horrified.

"Yeah," he says. "You were awake, off and on and the doctor came to see you. But, the cops and everyone else, especially me, thought it best to keep you at my house hidden."

"It is your house," I say.

"It is," he tells me, adding, by way of explanation, "I thought it was best that I get a house in town until all of the loose ends are wrapped up and then we'll go where you want to go. Or, we can leave it up to the boys, let them pick a random state and we'll try it out for as long as you want."

I nod and look at my hands, silently.

"What is it?" He asks.

"That's a really good offer," I tell him.

"Tell me you're not leaving," he says.

I look up at him and lean forward on my folded arms, and ask, "What would make you ask me that?"

John laughs, takes my hands, and says, "I know you, Ronnie. I know how protective you are and how strong you really are. Answer me this, how are you feeling?"

"Strange," I answer, honestly.

"Like you've woken from a bad dream or you've been released from a cage?" He asks, looking at my hands.

"Yeah," I tell him.

"And you don't know who you are," he says.

I take my hands gently from his and fold my arms across my chest before I tell him what I thought would be easier to admit out loud, "I'm sick. I know I am. I need therapy and medication. I am sick and I've been convincing myself for years that I'm not. Social security even admits that I'm sick. I get a check every month and still I've been pretending that I'm not sick. I use it to pay rent and I have just seen it as rent money. Not proof that there's anything wrong with me, but, there is something wrong with me."

He listens, quietly, and then asks, "What do you want to do?"

"Well," I tell him, putting my hands back on the table. And, then, thinking better of it, I pull out my dwindling cigarettes and light one. I continue, by saying, "There's the thing with Billy to take care of."

He nods and tells me, "All you have to do is file for divorce."

"What does that mean?" I ask.

"It means that I've been trying to prove to you how serious I am," John tells me, adding, "And, this has included putting his sorry ass in jail. He's facing about thirty years, thanks to the photos of what he did to you and they tested him and found nearly every drug under the sun, drugs on him, and many other things."

It's then that I notice the small bruise under his left eye and the question of his absence.

"Where have you been?" I ask. "And, what happened to your eye?"

And, then, I remember hitting someone when I was first brought to his house, in pain.

I ask, hand to my mouth, "I didn't hit you, did I?"

He laughs, "You remember hitting someone?"

"Yeah," I say, "Tell me it wasn't you."

"It wasn't," he says. "That was Joey and I still think that hilarious. But, that's just me. By the way, you knocked him out, cold cocked him, I loved it. You got a killer right hook, babe, you do. Makes me love you all the more."

"Love you too," I say, without thinking.

He doesn't miss it and looks over at me, a tiny smile on his face.

Then, he asks, "What's the problem then? So, you're sick. You've been through things that most people haven't been through and I don't know of anyone that could survive it without being on drugs or in a mental institution. I've waited for you for over twenty years. And, I've been through my own shit in the meantime. I can wait a little longer. But, I would feel better if you were safe, you and the boys. The house is ours. Yours. Live there. I'll be on the road, in and out and at least you'll have a home. I won't ask anything of you, like that. And, to be honest, after everything you've been through, I want to make love to you again. But, I can't do that to you right now. I know he raped you."

With that, I'm stunned into silence.

"I know," he continues. "He admitted it in his questioning. They allowed me to listen, to watch on video. He laughed about it, telling the cops that you belonged to him and it wasn't rape that he was taking back what was his. The cop in the room asked what that meant. I told him that you must have told him about us, without naming me."

I nod and look away.

"And, you were punished for it," he goes on. "Right. So, you want to know where I've been. Well, it seems I had a few traffic tickets and I caused a scene in the court. You know those chairs just fly around so randomly."

"You were purposely arrested?" I ask.

"You could say that," John tells me, proud of himself.

"And, the eye?" I ask.

"I taught someone a lesson," he says, adding, "Don't worry, he looks far worse than I do. And, he's scrambling to stop what he's facing and it's not going to happen. By the time they released me an hour ago, he's considering a plea of far less time, and more victims, like you, are emerging, most of them prostitutes of course, but, from the sounds of it, victims nonetheless."

I nod and look back at my hands.

"Say something," he presses.

"I don't know what to say," I tell him, honestly.

"Say you'll stay in the house," he tells me, adding, "I'll go on the road with the guys. You stay there, decide what you want to do, get therapy, medicine if you need it, and figure out who you are. Go back to school, paint, play music, write, do what makes you feel good about you. Figure it out, take your time. File for divorce, and I'll wait. When you're ready, I'll come back and hear the verdict. But, there you'll be safe and the boys will be safe. And, they'll be fed and you won't have to go to the streets again and it's up to you, the way it should have been throughout your life and never has been."

"Why are you doing this?" I ask.

"Because I love you," he tells me, "And, it's taken me this long to figure out what that truly means and when you love someone, you do what's best for them, like pushing them out the door when your life and wellbeing is in danger in favor of their career and their dreams."

He looks at me, slyly.

I smile to myself and look away, innocently.

John laughs and tells me, "If this is the way you want to do this, then I'll do it your way. Let me at least give you and the boys a roof over your head, please."

"What way do you want to do this?" I ask him.

He nods and says, "I'm glad you asked me that question. First off, let's silence the voices that have stained any relationship functioning. I'm not into groupies, I'm way too old for that shit anymore and I only have so much skin and t-shirts left."

I laugh and he looks at me and says, "You think I'm kidding, I'm not. I want to wake up in bed with someone that wants nothing more from me but my time, me. As broken and as damaged as you think you are, you are incredible person and honorable and just amazing."

I shake my head at him and look away.

"Right," he says, "Like I thought you would react. If you need a mirror, I'll be your mirror of what you are and who you are. And, if you want to know how I want to do this, I want to help you, be with you, through every step of making your life, our life together as amazing as it can be for as long as we have together, for as long as you want to be with me."

I still have no words.

"If you want to do this alone," he tells me, "You can, but, I want to be somewhere in your life. Not by email so that he doesn't find your phone. I don't want to be like your tricks or like Billy in your eyes."

"You're not," I tell him.

"I don't want to be your savior," he continues, "I don't want to be your knight in shining armor, because I'm not that either. I'm not. I'm as broken as you are, but, I've mended myself, through music, through time, through directing myself to where I need to be."

"I have to do that," I tell him.

"And, believe it or not," John tells me, "I can help you with that. I also don't want to be sitting here, sounding like I'm begging you for your attention."

"You're not," I tell him.

"Then," John continues, "I'm going to ask you something. What do you want me to do? I know no one has ever asked you that before, but, I'm asking now. What do you want me to do? Tell me, and whatever it is, I'll do it. Just tell me what you want me to do."

He's right. No one has ever asked me that question before. I don't know what to say. But, I take a moment and I think. My safe place has always been him, even before I knew it was him through the email. He was and always has been my safe place. And, I need my safe place. I need John. I need my boys. I need me.

How do I find me again?

I ask him, "Can you help me find me again?"

"I don't know," he tells me, adding, "But, I want to be there with you, while you're looking. And, I'll look with you. I promise you that."

"What do I do?" I ask him, stupidly.

"I can't tell you that, babe," he says. "And, I refuse to tell you what to do. But, the way I see it, you're standing on a cliff, looking down into nothing and Billy has made the decision to leave you and the boys on the cliff and dive off into nothingness. And, you need a safe place to jump." Safe place. "And, you can jump to me. I'll catch you. You know that. Everything else is up to you and what you want to do. But, I'm at the age now that I want the woman that is with me to actually want to be with me. Rather than to be with me because they have no other choice. Or, because I'm the best choice at the moment."

I nod and understand that I'm causing him pain by being as shattered as I am.

"John," I begin, "I'm not rejecting you. But, all I am is a whore, a fucking idiot, and I'm not good enough for my boys, let alone you. You deserve more than me, more than this fucking mess." And, the tears come and I can't stop them. "I just want to be more and I just know that someplace deep inside I can't be anything more for you. I don't want you to save me. I have to save me and my boys. I have to be more than that, more than what I've been in the past. And, I don't know how to do that."

He is silent for some time, sitting there. I wipe the tears from my eyes.

I continue, "You've always been my safe place. But, I have to be a safe place for my boys. How do I do that? How do I start again and give to you what you deserve? How do I do this? I don't know how to do this."

John licks his lips and looks at his hands.

Then, he says, "For everyone it's different. But, for me, I saw what I wanted for my future."

"What is that?" I ask.

"I want to be at peace," he tells me, "Waking up next to someone that wants to be there, wants to be with me because they know me and want to be with me and not some other fucked up reason."

"I want to be with you," I whisper.

"I know," he tells me, adding, "You just think you're not good enough to be there and it's me that's not good enough. I'll fail you, I will. I'll tell you this and I'm not trying to convince you of anything, I'm telling you how I feel." I nod. "When I saw you that day in the motel, going in with the guy, and I had been following you and watched you go off with three, four men, I was angry, I was heartbroken. I hadn't felt that way in many years. I just thought everything was gone. That everything was out of my hands. And, before I walked up to the motel room door, I called Mike and he told me that he had told you to push me away that day we spent together. He said, too, that the whole town knew that Billy had forced you to do this, that he was on drugs, that you weren't, but, you were trying to feed your boys. The whole town knew and was doing nothing about it. I've had music alone. I've had success alone. I'll trade it all away for that feeling you get when you go to bed at night and you worry over the ones in the house. That protective feeling. You have someone, you have people worth fighting for and it's not just you in the house. That feeling."

"I can't be perfect or good or even erase all that I've done," I tell him, honestly, "All I can do is try to be me. But, I want to be in my safe place. I want to touch your face again without feeling like you don't want me because I have the marks of a thousand other man's hands on my body."

He shakes his head and pulls my hand to him.

John tells me, "That's not why I didn't make love to you the other day. That's not why. I told you and I mean it, I don't want to hurt you. I don't want to be just another one of them."

"You're not," I tell him, adding, "And, if you're continually thinking that way, then maybe we can't do this."

"I'm not," he says, "But, I also don't want you to feel like you have to, going through the motions because you're paying me for something, like you owe me or something."

"No," I tell him. "You're the only one that I've been with like that. We made love and I wanted to do that again. Not pay you back or anything or be like I was. It wasn't like that, I swear."

"I also didn't want to physically hurt you," he tells me. "But, you have no idea of what I do want to give to you and be for you."

"Thank you," I tell him and decide that he's right, he is. Of course, anyone would have thought that I would just want or find that I needed to pay back with sex.

"What do you want to do?" He asks.

I think for a moment and ask him, "Can we go home?"

He smiles and says, "I like the sound of that."

I nod and tell him, "I have to make a stop first, a couple of stops."

"Of course," John tells me.

Together, we gather a few things for the boys and myself. And, then, we lock up the house. In the car, I direct him to the courthouse, and there I file for divorce. When I go to file for a restraining order, I find out there's already one in place. That day, that very hour in the courthouse, I'm granted full custody of the boys. And, suddenly, a load lifts from my shoulders. When I get back into the car, I realize what that load is.

"If you ever doubt how I feel about you," I tell John as he drives away, "Just know that you're the only one that has ever entered my life, outside of the boys, that I haven't felt that I was forced to take care of. You're not a burden to me. You and the boys are the only ones that have never been a burden."

John stops the car, pulls off to the side of the road, sits there a moment and thinks.

"What's the matter?" I ask, worried I've said something wrong.

He shakes his head, tells me, "Nothing. Absolutely nothing."

He takes a moment, pulls the car back into traffic and takes me back to our home. There, I make several calls, to a doctor and a therapist, making appointments with them, and the last call I make is to my landlord. I tell him what has happened and that we're moving out and going elsewhere. I'll be taking those things we need and nothing more. The rest of it I can't take with me. He understood and said he would be heading to the house the next day to change the locks and everything, if that's when I wanted to take care of it. I agree and thank him and get off the phone.

I sit back and think and look over at John who is sitting there, in the living room, on the couch, in the house he has bought for us. The only thing left to do is to get the boys.

I tell John, "Now let's get the boys, right?"

He leans forward, rests his hands on his knees, and tells me, "Tomorrow."

"Why tomorrow?" I ask.

"Because," he says, standing, "I would like to hold you tonight and be near you all night, all alone. If that's alright with you?"

I nod, tears in my eyes.

We go to the room and to bed, wrapped in one another. We talk and whisper and I tell him about what I've gone through in the past few months, how the memory of our time together has helped me make it through. We fall asleep and wake in the middle of the night to make love and we sleep again.

The next day, I rush to my boys and can't let go of them once I have them.

Every moment is shaky and I hold onto John and the boys with both hands, refusing to let them go. When I do see the therapist, he listens and tells me that medicine will work and that I'm a good mom. It's that small encouragement that lifts me from my hole, higher than anything else has.

I am a different person after that. Medicine comes and the quirk is named again and put at bay. It isn't in control anymore. And, John and I take a day at a time, walk this through together, with the boys happy and growing. Billy goes to jail and his junkies are in and out constantly.

The divorce is finally finalized and we sit at the table, talking one night about where we want to go. And, we decide on a random state and move the next day, pulling up the already yanked up roots and move on. As we leave the state, I take off my shoes and toss them out the window.

John laughs. He tells the boys, "Boys, your mother has an excellent plan. Throw your shoes out the window." The boys laugh and take their shoes off and toss them out the window. He then takes his off, while driving and throws them out too. He turns to me, then, and says, "If my brother wants to see us, I guess he'll be coming to us."

"Right," I tell him, and all of us laugh.

Made in United States
Troutdale, OR
11/13/2024

24745441R00149